P9-DVK-436

JAKE RILEY

IRREPARABLY DAMAGED

JAKE RILEY
IRREPARABLY DAMAGED

Rebecca Fjelland Davis

HarperTempest
An Imprint of HarperCollins*Publishers*

www.harperchildrens.com

Library of Congress Cataloging-in-Publication Data
Davis, Rebecca Fjelland.
   Jake Riley : irreparably damaged / by Rebecca Fjelland
Davis.
      p.   cm.
   Summary: The friendship between a troubled boy,
recently released from a reform school, and the farm girl
who lives next door angers the faculty at their school and
leads to a dangerous confrontation.
   ISBN 0-06-051837-5 —ISBN 0-06-051838-3 (lib. bdg.)
   [1. Friendship—Fiction. 2. Emotional problems—Fiction.
3. High schools—Fiction. 4. Schools—Fiction. 5. Farm
life—Fiction.] I. Title.
PZ7.D2977 Jak 2003   2002014417
[Fic]—dc21   CIP
                                                  AC

Typography by Lizzy Bromley
1 3 5 7 9 10 8 6 4 2

First Edition

For Nikki and Josh
for being and for being who you are.

And for all my other kids:
Anissa and Pascal,
Daniel and Stephanie,
Noelle, Derek, Leah, Kaia, Reid, Lindsay, Katie, and Ty.

Thanks to Terry, for endless reasoning.
To George Nicholson and Mark McVeigh for changing my life.

CHAPTER 1

In summer the fireflies live by the millions in the oats field. Their lights blink on and off when we run after them, and our arms and legs look choppy, like we're stick men playing tag in strobe lights. They blink their get-away turns into the dark, but some aren't so lucky.

Jake says you have to pull them apart while their lights are on, "'cause if you *disembowel* them with their lights off, they'll never go back on." Disembowel. I think *disembowel* is the only big word he knows.

I wonder how many nerves are in their little bodies when we catch them with their lights on, rip off their glowing bellies, and stick the lights to our fingers. They shine a few long minutes before their batteries wear out. I always wonder if the other part of each bug keeps kicking as long as its light shines on my finger. But I never look for the dead parts to find out.

I say that if we're going to disembowel some bugs,

we should do it to obnoxious bugs like mosquitoes and yellow jackets.

Jake tries to give me a kick in the shin, but I'm too fast for him. "Stupid," he says, "this is what lightning bugs are for."

I think maybe they're just for us to look at, little fallen stars scooting around the oats field. So I feel guilty ripping their glowing life from them, but not guilty enough to stop. It's the same feeling I have when we take cattle or pigs or sheep to market so somebody can eat them, after I've named all of them.

Jake chases me through the oats as if we're little kids. We laugh and wave our bright, jeweled hands so they make glowing yellow arcs in the night, like pale sparklers. We run faster, and some of the glowing jewels slip from our fingers; others cling until they're lifeless and dark.

The stalks and heads of grain make tiny paper cuts on our arms and legs. I can run faster than Jake; I have long skinny legs, and he's squatty and has a belly. Sometimes I let him catch me anyway, because he gets so mad when I always beat him.

We run, then he tackles me, and we fly headlong into the oats. We laugh, and he hangs on when I try to roll away. "Jake," I say, "let go, we're smashing the oats."

We roll around enough to flatten a little room. "My dad'll kill us," I say, but Jake won't let go. I try to punch him, but he's got my arms pinned. When he lets go, he laughs and we flop back, gazing up at the stars.

"If you looked down at this oats field," I say, "it would look like those pictures in science books that are cut right though the middle of ant hills to show how they're made. Lots of tunnels connecting little rooms."

Jake says, "Don't know what you mean, smarty-pants."

He wouldn't. He's got no imagination, and I don't try to explain it to him.

Jake's looking at me in the dark. When I look at him, he reaches over and whips my shirt up to my armpits.

"Don't!" I yell. I jerk up my knees, and one whacks him hard in the hip. My knee's pretty bony, so he lets go of me real fast, and I jump up.

"You're gettin' big," he says. "Nice." He's grinning in the moonlight, teeth glowing like a jack-o'-lantern.

I pull my shirt tight against my ribs. "I hate you!" I say. "I hate you!" And I turn and run, cutting a new tunnel through the oats anthill.

I stay away from Jake for five days. It's hard in the

summer, with nobody else around who's our age. I miss having him to talk to, but every time I'm getting dressed or taking a bath, I think about him yanking my shirt up and exposing my nipples to the night air.

We both have to help with the oats combining in August. My dad owns this big farm. It takes up a whole section: "Six hundred forty acres of black Iowa dirt, and we can farm six hundred ten of it," he always says.

Jake's dad works the night shift at Matsco Machine shop in Slater. He has rented the other house on our land for two years, and Dad cuts him a deal because he helps us with fieldwork all through the growing season. In April, Jake came to live with his dad permanently.

In March, Raymond Riley had told Dad, "My boy's coming to live with me. So there'll be two of us in the house. He's been in a little trouble, and his mom can't handle him." Dad told me that he had looked Raymond in the eye and said, "What kind of trouble?" Raymond said, "A pretty serious fight. Got sent to the reform school in Eldora for it."

I asked Jake about it later, about why he got sent there, and he said, "for fighting." That's it. That's all we know. Raymond's not much for talking, and Jake hasn't been in any trouble around here that I know of. The only things I know about Jake's mom is that she doesn't live with his dad anymore and that we've never seen her.

I help my dad in the field, and Jake helps his dad hauling wagons to the bin and unloading them, so he only sees me long enough to call me "smarty-pants."

I'm a little nervous that Dad will see the smashed oats where Jake and I tromped it down.

Sure enough, I'm riding with him in the combine cab and he says, "You responsible for that flat patch, Lainey?"

"Guess so."

"'S about half a peck of oats smashed."

"I'm sorry, Dad."

"Combine can't pick that up, Lainey. That's a pure waste."

I study the oats washing into the combine head.

"What were you doin' out there?"

"Nothing. Goofin' around. Just goofin' with Jake." I think about Jake jerking my shirt up, and I feel my face get hot. I press my nose against the cool glass of the combine window, and I study real carefully how the oats look like a golden waterfall going up into the reel of the combine head. I'm glad Dad can't see inside my head like there's a video screen in there and the sides of my head are glass, all glass like the combine cab.

"I reckon you can pitch out the hen house to pay for the oats."

"The whole hen house?" I ask.

Cleaning the hen house is the worst. Pig manure is stinky and sloppy, and sheep manure is like trying to peel manure-flavored Fruit Roll-Ups off the barn floor with a shovel, but chicken manure turns to pure dust. You breathe it, you cough it, it gets in your hair and your eyes, and you can't get it out of your throat for days.

"Yup," he says.

"Jake has to help," I say.

"What's Jake got to do with it?"

I think about him pinning me and me telling him to let me up, but I don't say that. I just say, "He did it, too."

Dad sighs and turns the combine to skirt the drainage ditch.

"Listen, Lainey," he says, "you know better. I'm not sure Jake has the sense he was born with. I think some got knocked out of him, and he's a good-for-nothin' except when his daddy's makin' him work like now." Dad nods in the direction of the grain bin. "You're responsible for what happens to you. You let him talk you into something, it's your fault. I'm not responsible for raisin' Jake right. It's too late for that. But you—you have to clean the chicken house."

The grain hopper's full, so I climb out of the cab and move the tractor so the wagon is positioned under the combine auger. Then Dad yells over the avalanche of grain, "Time for lunch. You go get it. Mom should have it ready."

Mom packed enough for Jake and Raymond, too, so we all take a break and eat minced-ham sandwiches and chocolate cupcakes with fluffy frosting and drink lemonade together at the fencerow. Jake's dad says the beans look better than they have for seven years. Dad squints at the bean field, next to us, and nods. I don't look at Jake. Not once. He doesn't say anything to me, either.

One night after combining, Jake comes over after dark with his rifle.

"Lainey-Belainey," he says through the screen door, "wanna go shoot coons in the slough?"

"No," I say. I've just recently quit smelling chicken manure in my hair.

"They're eatin' sweet corn left and right," he says. "And my dad says some highfalutin guy from a museum in Kansas City is in town, payin' twenty-five dollars a pelt. Gonna make authentic coonskin caps, I guess."

I think about the Levi's I want for school that Mom says are too expensive, and I say, "Okay," and I get Dad's .22.

"Mom," I yell, "Jake and I are going coon huntin'."

"You be careful," she says.

The door slams behind me.

We don't talk. We just walk with our rifles slung in the crooks of our arms. I think we probably look like Tom Sawyer and Becky Thatcher, or maybe more like Tom and Huck Finn, because I've got on old cutoff jeans and one of Dad's old work shirts, and my hair is short enough to pass for a boy's. Jake's black hair is thin and straight and about an inch and a half past haircut stage. He keeps tossing it out of his eyes.

"Sorry I did that to ya," he says.

I look at him funny. All the times he's hurt me or made me mad, he's never apologized. "What?" I say.

"You know," he says.

I know exactly what he means, but I want to hear him say it.

"You know," he says. "Yank your shirt up like that, look at your tits."

I feel my face getting red in the moonlight. Nobody

ever called them that before. I kick a dirt clod, hard.

"Why'd you do such a stupid thing?" I ask.

Jake shrugs. "Dunno. Don't want you to hate me."

"Then you shouldn't have done it." I keep looking down, feeling his eyes on me.

"I just . . ." he starts to say, then kicks a clod himself. "I just wanted to see what they looked like. I could see 'em under your shirt, and I wanted to feel 'em, but I knew you wouldn't let me so I wanted to at least sneak a look."

"Jerk," I say. "You got no right. You don't see me pullin' your pants down to get a look at your puny dick."

"How do you know it's puny? It's not." He shoves me.

"Stop it, moron. We got loaded guns."

"Don't care. It's not puny. Want me to prove it? I'd be glad to show ya." He sets down his gun, leans the barrel against a maple tree, unsnaps, and starts unzipping his jeans.

"No way, you sicko!" I aim my gun at his crotch. "You show it to me, and I'll shoot it."

"Jesus!" he says. He zips up quick and we walk in silence.

The slough is real dark, but the moon is shining. It smells of the rotting plant-flesh of cattails, moss, and swamp grass. It's too wet to farm, so it's a haven for every creature that lives in central Iowa. The sweet corn field comes right up next to the slough. Dad says planting the sweet corn here is like putting it on a plate for the coons, but he doesn't have much choice because sweet corn has a shorter growing season than anything else we raise, and the land here is usually too wet to plant until late in the spring.

We walk, quiet as can be, and we hear the cornstalks rattling. We crouch in the tall weeds at the edge of the field and cock our guns.

A big fat one comes waddling out of the corn and we both aim. "'S mine," Jake whispers. He blasts and it rolls over, blood pulsing from the neck, but it still scrabbles toward the grass. Jake blasts again, and it lies still, bleeding from the shoulder, too.

"Hope they can still make a hat outa it," I say.

"Aim for the head or the neck," Jake says.

The cornstalks are silent. We can't see any coons, but we know they are hanging on for dear life right now, staring from the cornstalks out of their bandit masks at the big noise and gunpowder smell. Jake and I don't move a muscle.

Finally, one runs from between the rows toward the slough. Jake aims but lets me shoot. I'm a good shot, and the coon's eye sort of pops, bloody, out of his head, and he stops with his head turned sideways into the furrow like a jackknifed truck.

We stay, patient, until way after midnight. Jake gets three coons, and I get two. By the time we come home, swinging our money by the tail, our legs are so full of cramps that we can hardly walk for the first half mile.

The next week, I buy my Levi's.

CHAPTER 2

One morning during the first week of ninth grade, I'm wearing my new jeans, walking with my two best friends, Amy and Jailene. Amy's telling us how Peter Stortman got fed up with how snotty Meredith Baker was in art class yesterday and "accidentally" dumped paint in her hair on the way to his table. "I think even Mr. Reed thought she had it coming," she says. Jailene laughs so hard she snorts.

Jake comes out of the industrial technology education room just as we turn the corner. He looks okay: dark hair cut and not greasy at all, not falling over his face but combed, with a new-looking Harley-Davidson T-shirt tucking his paunch into not-too-dirty jeans, and Nikes that his coon money paid for. His eyes are on the floor until he spies me. His head comes up.

Jake didn't start school last spring, because he came to live with his dad so late in the school year. Amy and

Jailene never got a good look at him any time they were at my house this summer.

"Lainey-Belainey," he says. That's what he calls me when he's glad to see me.

Amy and Jailene converge at my ears, hands cupped, both talking into different sides of my head at the same time.

"Is that *Jake*?"

"Yup," I say.

"That's the Jake you've been telling us about?" Amy says. Your neighbor? He's old, isn't he? He looks too old to be a freshman. Laine, do you *like* him?"

"No!" I say. "I don't *like* him. And yes, he's a freshman. Not that old."

I think maybe Jake looks old because his eyes look old, pale blue, like my grandpa's used to, as if he's been alive a long, long time. But Amy and Jailene aren't looking at his eyes. They just see a boy's body that's thick enough all the way up and down to look strong, instead of fat like I know he really is. His dark hair is so freshly cut that there's pale skin then a tan line all around the bottom of it.

Jake looks at me, and his pale eyes aren't happy. Like he's mad at me for saying that I don't like him.

"Hey, sugar pie," Jake says.

"Don't call me that, Jake."

Amy pokes me hard in the ribs. "Why didn't you tell us?"

I give her a look intended to kill, but Amy and Jailene convulse in giggles. Amy's long yellow hair falls around her face while she laughs. Jake's looking at her hair. It's so pretty, it's hard to miss.

"Hey, smarty-pants," he says to me.

"Sugar pie!" Amy screams through her laughter. "Smarty-pants!"

I smack her in the shoulder. "Shut up, Jake," I say through my teeth. "Come on, you guys." I grab Amy's and Jailene's elbows so hard they squawk. I feel like I'm dragging two chickens by their wings.

"Got your coon jeans on, I see," he yells after me, and I yank Amy and Jailene down the hall.

"He's kinda cute," Jailene says.

"Naw, he's kinda fat," Amy says.

"Do you like him, Lainey?" Jailene asks.

"Shut up!" I say, and we escape into Mr. Eikton's English class.

I like English because we do so many different things, plus I have it with both Amy and Jailene. We don't talk to each other in that class though, because

Eikton has everybody's respect. On Mondays, Wednesdays, and Fridays, we have spelling tests. We've been talking about the sounds of words and syllables, and he's making us read some poetry. Most everybody hates it. I don't, but I don't tell anybody that. Every day for the first eight minutes, we have free reading. Eikton lets us read whatever we want, as long as he okays it. That means books or magazine articles. No junk. I'm starting *To Kill a Mockingbird* because it's on the suggested reading list. Eikton says we'd like it.

Today, Amy's reading an article from *Sassy* magazine, and if that doesn't qualify as junk, I don't know what would, so I guess the no-junk rule is pretty loosely enforced. Jailene's reading a paperback romance from the library. Most of the front cover is consumed by a picture of cleavage.

There's a new girl in our class with a nosering named Arcadia Knowles who's been reading articles every day from a magazine called *Muscle & Fitness* with a guy on the front who has biceps as big as my waist. People have been giving her weird looks, but either she hasn't noticed or she doesn't care.

"What's the big deal?" Jake asks through my screen door that night. He's standing on the squeaky board of our porch, jiggling up and down for effect.

"What do you mean, what's the big deal?" I ask. I get up from the table where I'm trying to multiply negative integers for Mr. Pragman's class.

My mom's ironing in the kitchen, so I go out the screen door and let it bang shut. "Don't slam that door," she yells.

"What are you, too good for me?" he says as we go down the steps to the yard. "Can't talk to me at school?"

"Well, why'd you call me such stupid names?"

"Why'd you say you don't like me?"

"'Cause they meant like a boyfriend, dummy." I say the word *dummy* softly. For once it seems to matter that I don't hurt his feelings.

"You showed me your tits, didn't you?"

"I did not!" I whirl on him and swing my fist at his head. He's not ready, and even though he jerks back his head, I feel his nose bend and blood on my knuckles.

"You little shit! You think you're so great!" He grabs my shoulders and shoves me down backward. The dirt is hard, and I can't get a breath. The pebbles scrape my back and my tailbone, and I roll over onto my stomach. Jake jumps on top of me, bouncing on my back.

"Stop it! What are you doing? My back's wet!"

"I'm bleeding on you," he says. "You sure are strong

for somebody so skinny." He puts his hand on my triceps.

I kick, trying to get him in the back with my heels, but he's sitting on the small of my back, and my heels hit only air.

"Get off me," I say. "You're gettin' blood on me!"

"Be quiet. You want your mom to come out here?" He touches my arm again. "You're real strong. But I guess I can still hold ya down."

I quit struggling. He runs his hands over my back. It feels almost nice. I like it, and I hate that I like it. I think of how he looked at Amy's hair today.

"Did I hurt you?" he asks.

I think about what Dad said about it being too late to raise him right. "I guess not as much as I hurt you," I say. "Let me up. Now."

"Wait," he says softly. "You feel nice. Hey, you got a bra on. How come you only wear one some of the time?"

"None of your business, Jake. Let me go."

He traces my bra line with his finger. I smash my arms against my sides so his finger can't go any farther around me than across my back.

"Wanna be my girlfriend?" he says.

"Jake, let me up."

"You never wore a bra last summer," he says.

"It was too hot, you jerk. I almost never wear one in the summer. What's it to you, anyway? Now let me up."

"Tell me."

"What?" I say.

"If you'll be my girlfriend. If you'll like me that way."

I stop fighting. "I'll think about it, if you let me up."

He gets off, and I jump up. He scuffs the ground with his toe.

"Jake," I say, my heart pounding, "I just wanna be friends. Don't wanna be your girlfriend."

"You said . . ."

"I said I'd think about it." I'm running around the house and up the steps, inside and banging the screen door before he's even to the porch.

"Don't bang that door," Mom says. "How many times do I have to tell you?"

I hook the door and press my nose against the squares of the screen as Jake comes up the steps two at a time.

"See ya tomorrow, Jake," I say with lips in the tiny squares. "You can wash your face at the pump if you want." I duck into the kitchen, but I leave the porch light on for him.

"Lainey!" Mom says. "You've got blood all over!

What'd you do to your back?"

"Nothing, Mom. Jake bled on me."

"On your back? How on earth? What are you doing at your age, roughhousing like that with a boy?"

"Mom!"

"Look at your jeans. Your new jeans."

I crane to look at my rear end. There is a little hole scraped above the left back pocket of my Levi's. I hate Jake.

CHAPTER 3

My dad and Jake's dad are each driving a truck to Chicago for Meyer and Sons at the elevator. They've got to clear out last year's soybeans to make space for people to start bringing in this year's beans. Mom told Jake he could eat at our house while his dad's gone.

"Mom! Why'd you invite him? I don't want to look at his face for two breakfasts and two suppers. Can I stay at Jailene's for supper tonight? Please?"

"You'll do no such thing," Mom says.

After school, and after a tough cross-country practice, and after doing chores with Mom, I'm trying to write a haiku for Mr. Eikton's class. It's not working. He's talked about how good poetry makes the reader look at things differently. So far my first line is:

running like a deer

Nothing different about that. I've heard it before, in the John Deere ad for starters, but I want to write about running because it's the only thing I know I do well. I'm on our school's small cross-country team, and today, the high-school track coach, Ms. Barks—who's also the phys ed teacher—told me she hopes I'll train for spring track through the winter. I said I'd plan on it.

I want to run like nobody ever ran before. Sometimes I feel like the wind wraps around my legs and nothing can catch me. Last year, I ran the 400 and 800, and I got first in all but one junior-high meet. Our 4 x 400 relay team placed every time, too. The coach talked about me running the mile this year. I don't know. She says a person can win at the junior-high level with enough natural ability, but this year on varsity, I'll have to work because our conference has produced lots of state champions. I want to go to state.

Last year, Dad wasn't too thrilled about the whole deal, because Mom had to drive into town to pick me up every day after practice during planting season. I'm going out for track if it kills me—and it just might, if I have to walk the whole five miles home from school after practice every day. Now that I'm in high school, though, there's an activity bus after practice. That gives me an idea, though, and I write:

the wind wraps around my legs

There. That's seven syllables and it would work for the middle line. We have to have three of these haiku things done for tomorrow, and it's taking a lot more time than I thought it would.

I am reaching for the book with examples of haikus in it when Jake says through the screen door, "Lainey-Belainey, whatcha doin'?"

I jump. "Jeez," I say. "You heard of knocking?"

Jake shrugs. "Come here."

"What? I'm busy. Doin' homework. Don't you ever have homework?"

"Naw."

"What are you doing here, anyway? Supper's not 'til six."

"Got somethin' to show ya."

"What?"

"Come see." He's smirking with that you-won't-believe-this-but-when-you-see-it-you'll-think-I'm-cool look, sort of like James Dean's face on the posters at Video Magic. Too bad Jake's chubby face doesn't look like good ol' J.D. But then, if he looked like that, my answer might have been a lot different when Jailene and Amy asked if I liked him.

I put down my mechanical pencil and followed him outside. We walk, hands in our pockets, toward his house.

"I hate school," he says.

"Maybe you wouldn't if you did some homework."

"Who cares? I'm hopeless."

"Who says you're hopeless?" I ask. I think of what Dad said in the combine about it being too late to raise Jake right, and my stomach feels like somebody's squeezing it.

"Ir-repair-ably damaged. That's what I am."

"Irreparably?" I say, pronouncing it better than he did. "Where'd you hear that?"

"In Mrs. Prebyl's office. That's what my file says. I saw it."

"The counselor? She has a file on you?"

He nods. His hair hangs in black spikes above his eyebrows when it isn't combed, which is most of the time, and I think about how much fun he can be when he's not being a jerk, and I almost want to hug him, want him to know that he doesn't have to be a total loser. I'm not about to hug him, though, so all I do is kick a stone on the edge of the lane. I'm a pretty good shot kicking, too. Too bad we don't have a soccer team.

Jake brings me into the living room and makes me

sit on the couch that's in the middle of the room to divide it from the dining room.

"Close your eyes," he says.

"Why are you damaged? Irreparably damaged?" I ask with my eyes shut. This place stinks, like mildew and dust and rotten fruit in the garbage. I guess he and his dad don't clean very much.

"Never mind," he says. I feel the cool, slick paper of a magazine in my hands. "Look," he says from behind me.

I look. There's a naked man and woman, touching and kissing each other. I feel all exposed, like it's my body there, and Jake's looking over my shoulder at me naked. But it's not my body, it's a beautiful one, all blossomed and full and ripe.

"You're gonna look like that," he says. "You sorta do now." I want to shove the magazine away, but I can't take my eyes off it. Jake leans over my shoulder, sees me looking, and smiles. I can hear my dad's voice saying, *You let him talk you into something, it's your fault.* It's my fault that I'm here.

I look at it too long before I push it away. "Where'd you get this?" I ask.

"In the mail. Now I know why Dad always gets the mail."

"I'm going home." I jump up, but he climbs over the couch and grabs me from behind by both arms. "Let me go, Jake."

"No, wait."

The squeeze in my stomach is back.

"Let's try it," he says. "No one will ever know."

"You're crazy!" I fight against him, but he's holding me tight. "Stop it, you're hurting my elbows."

He slips his arms around me so he's pinning my arms against my ribs, and he presses against me from behind. It feels like maybe he unzipped his jeans while I had my eyes shut.

"You sicko!" I yell. "Maybe you *are* hopeless."

"You can do that—like that picture—with me and I'd know I'm not . . . damaged . . . and that you like me. That a girl wants to do it with me."

"I'll never, ever, do that with you in a million years!"

"Everybody does."

Everybody. I think of my mom and dad. "Not everybody, you moron. I'm *not* doing it with you!" The more I fight, the more I feel him against me, and I can't get away. "You're not damaged, you're deranged!" I scream at him.

"Before I came to live with my dad," Jake says, still holding me, "I was in reform school in Eldora. I lived with all boys, mostly bigger than me."

While he's talking, Jake is squeezing tighter, like he's remembering and not paying attention to what he's doing. "I hated it there. If I got damaged, that's where it was. They—the bigger boys—they made me . . ." He squeezes so tight I think I hear my ribs crack.

"Jake, don't," I say. "That hurts." I know I have to do something before he does crack my ribs. "You hated them, didn't you? Those boys, I mean?" I ask.

"Yeah, I guess," he whispers in my neck, and his grip relaxes ever so slightly.

I breathe a little easier. "So, if you hated them, don't do this to me, or I'll hate you, too. Jake, please?"

He lets go just a little, and I jerk away. I'm at the door. He comes after me and grabs for my arm, but I push through the door, jump over the step, and run.

He runs after me, but he can't catch me. "You tell anyone," he screams after me, "I'll kill you. I swear, I'll shoot you through your bedroom window with my twenty-two!"

I'm running, faster than I've ever run in a track meet.

CHAPTER 4

He comes over for supper anyway and we don't look at each other or say a single word to each other. He's very polite to Mom and she keeps trying to get a conversation going with him, but it's hopeless. She knows she's beaten when she asks, "Do you ever hear from your mother?"

He takes a big bite of stew and shakes his head without looking at her. I can tell this is working Mom's motherly sympathies, and I can hardly swallow. I can't wait until he's gone.

Finally, we clear the table, and Jake asks me to walk him home.

"No way, you pervert," I say.

"Lainey! You don't talk to a guest that way," Mom says.

"Only to perverts," I say.

"Lainey!" Mom looks like she's ready to smack me

across the mouth, so even though I want to say, *You should hear what he said to his guest this afternoon*, of course I don't say it.

Jake smirks at me. He knows he's got me, and I hate him.

"Jake," Mom says, "you got laundry that needs doing? Bring it over and I'll do it for you."

"Mom!" I say. "His dad'll be home in a couple days."

"I'm bein' neighborly, Lainey. You be quiet. Here, Jake, put your dirty clothes in this." She hands him a garbage bag. She hands me a dish towel.

"Poor kid," she says when he's out the door.

"Hardly," I say. She ignores me.

We're finishing the dishes when Jake comes back. He walks right in and closes the screen door gently so it doesn't bang.

"Knock, you pervert," I say.

"Lainey," Mom says as if she's tired.

"Well, he is." I see the wrinkles around her eyes, and sometimes I wonder if I'm the reason for them.

"I'll do this laundry for you while you're in school tomorrow," Mom says. "Lainey, he's got to go home to an empty house. Walk him home."

"No. Besides, he was just there."

"Now," she says.

I hate her for making me.

I let the screen door bang, and I walk so fast that Jake has to almost trot to keep up with me. He's huffing.

"You're an asshole," I say. "Once I thought you were my friend."

"You think I'm gay?" he asks.

"Jeez! How would I know?"

"Because I told you what happened to me, and I've only done it with guys. But I'd like to do it with you, so that makes me not gay."

"Jeez!" I walk even faster.

"Doesn't it?" he huffs.

"What?"

"Wanting to do it with you makes me not gay, right?"

"It doesn't make me your girlfriend! And it doesn't make me like you *that way*." I don't want to talk about this, so I turn around so fast my running shoe leaves a spin mark in the gravel, and I'm gone. I get home and inside the house in record time.

"I've told you a million times," Mom says. "Don't bang that door."

Finally, finally, I can work on my haikus again. I want to write about running, or about the wind in the slough grass, but all I can think about is Jake. I look at the poem I started before supper, and the last two lines come to me:

the wind wrapped around my legs
and Jake can't catch me

I need a first line. Finally I write:

I want to run free
with wind wrapped around my legs
so Jake can't catch me

I still need two more haikus. I try to think about something "picturesque" from my life. I try:

combine picks up grain

then:

combine swallows grain
like a yellow waterfall

I cross that out. Gold, gold. Oats are like gold. I've got to use that.

combine swallows grain
like the mouth of a miser
eating all the gold

That one was almost too easy, and I like it the best. Combining makes me think of Dad saying that it's too late to raise Jake right, and then I think about this afternoon. I wonder if I told Mom, if Jake would really come and shoot me. I don't think he'd have the guts, but he can get really crazy, and I still don't know about the fight that sent him to reform school. That gives me the creeps. Maybe I can tell Mom what Jake did today and she'll let me sleep with her until Dad gets back. I could put pillows under my blankets so if Jake came, that's what he would shoot. But I doubt she'd let me. If Dad thinks that it's my fault if I let Jake talk me into something, Mom would think so, too. So, I write:

fly in a cobweb

I hate him. I think about him holding me so tight it hurt. I wish I could kick him in the balls right now. Then I think about what he said, and I wonder if he got beat up a lot at the boys' home. And I wonder how it happened, if some big guys ganged up on him, or if one big boy just scared him into doing whatever it was. Thinking about it makes me gag. I write:

fly in a cobweb
kick and struggle, kick and fight
finally buzz free

We're both flies, Jake and me.

My palms are all sweaty and my neck is stiff, like I've been fighting him off while I sit still in this chair.

I'm tired of thinking so much, so I curl up in bed and read more of *To Kill a Mockingbird*.

CHAPTER 5

Our dads get back on Tuesday night, so Jake can eat at his own house again. "Chicago," Dad says, "is too big and too fast and too dirty around the edges for me." He grins at me over his orange juice on Wednesday morning. "But we got to see the Cubs game."

"Lucky," I say through my teeth. "How come you didn't take me?"

"Those poor Cardinals," Dad says. "They didn't know what hit them. I couldn't take you. You'd have felt sorry for them."

"Not," I say.

"But I did bring you something." He throws me a Cubs T-shirt.

"Thanks, Dad!" I skip stairs going up to my room to put it on. I'm a big Cubs fan. Since Iowa doesn't have a major league baseball team, we all adopt somebody from a neighboring state. Jake likes the Cardinals because his grandpa, Raymond's dad, lives in St. Louis and has taken Jake to a few games. Jailene and Amy are only fair-weather fans, so they like the Twins because they have won a World Series recently. The best thing about liking the Cubs is that their minor league team ("farm team," as Dad calls it), the Iowa Cubs, are in Des Moines, and sometimes we go watch them. When Dad was little, they were the Iowa Oaks, a minor league team for Oakland, and Dad has told me ten times that he went to a game when Vida Blue pitched the whole thing plus hit five home runs, one of which Dad caught. The next season, Vida Blue was playing for the Oakland A's, and I always got the feeling Dad felt partially responsible for Vida Blue's success. I only remember when Vida Blue retired, and I think it made Dad feel real old.

I'm waiting for the bus a little later when Jake comes galumphing up the shoulder of the road with his Nikes untied so they slop with every step. The bus stops at his house, too, but sometimes he can't stand being over there, where he can see me a quarter mile away and not get to bug me. His hair is still wet from the shower, so at least he's clean, but I can see orange juice pulp in the corners of his mouth.

"Mornin', Lainey-Belainey," he says.

"Wipe your mouth," I say.

He quickly swipes it with the back of one hand, embarrassed.

"Look what my dad brought me," he says, holding up an ivory-handled pocketknife with the other hand.

"Neat," I say. "My dad brought me this shirt." I open my jean jacket, grab the bottom edges of the white T-shirt, and hold it out so he can read CHICAGO CUBS in Technicolor script without having to look too closely at my breasts.

"Let's see the knife," I say, holding out my hand, and Jake drops it in.

"Let's see the shirt," Jake says, holding out his hands.

"Very funny," I say, turning my back and looking down the road for the bus, but it's not coming yet. "They'll take this away if they find out you have it in school, you know."

"Nobody's gonna know," Jake says, "unless of course Miss Smarty-Pants herself tells 'em."

"Right," I say. "If I were tellin' on you, I'd have told worse stuff a long time ago."

He kicks a piece of gravel across the highway.

I flip out the knife blades and wave them at him like

I'm Edward Scissorhands. I say, "So don't try that crap on me again, okay?"

The beginning of a smile touches his lips, and I can see he's relieved to know I haven't told.

A motor roars toward us, too sporty and way too fast for the bus, but I close the knife fast and hand it back. It's the red Camaro that belongs to Jim Pietzman, the veterinarian's son. He's a senior this year. He got the car for his eighteenth birthday.

There's a gray squirrel in the middle of the road, frozen, scared to death to move either way, and I cry out when I see the spinning black tires go right over the back end of him. The red car zooms away, and the squirrel screams and screams, like normal squirrel chatter in one long, uninterrupted shriek.

Jake runs to the squirrel and reaches out his hand, but it tries to bite him, and he jerks his hand back just in time. The squirrel tries to drag his hindquarter away, but he can't. It's plastered to the pavement.

"Lainey," Jake says, "we can't leave him here. He'll get smashed."

"He's already smashed, Jake."

"I mean completely. He's gonna lay here and suffer 'til somebody flattens him."

"Maybe that'd put him out of his misery," I say.

"If the bus doesn't get him, that could be a couple hours!" Jake yells at me, his voice like a fist. "There's not much traffic on this road. We're not gonna leave him . . ."

"Well, what do you plan on doin'? Should we shoot him?"

"Yeah, maybe," Jake says.

We watch the squirrel trying to curl up to see its leg better, biting at it as if that might make it come loose from the pavement. I feel sick.

"That gives me an idea," Jake says. "Maybe we don't have to shoot him. You ever heard of wolves chewing off their own legs that are stuck in traps?" He pulls out his pocketknife. "If I had some string," he says, "I could tie off his leg and cut it off."

"You're crazy!"

"That's what they did in Civil War hospitals."

"What?" I say.

"In the movies," Jake says. "Haven't you ever seen it? Like in *The Blue and the Gray*? This way he'll die for sure. He'd never be able to drag that dead leg up a tree. But without it, he could climb a tree again. There are three-legged dogs out there doing just fine." His face is a little white. "I'd have to tie it tight," he says. "Otherwise, he'd bleed to death."

I imagine cutting through that bone and that torn-up

muscle with just a pocketknife. I'm not crazy about cutting through freshly butchered chicken meat and muscle, but the thought of cutting through living tissue makes me want to puke.

"Go get some string," Jake orders. "Your mom's got some."

"Jake, the bus is coming." We can hear the roar as it turns the corner down the highway and accelerates toward us.

"Go get the string. You got time," he says.

I leave my backpack at the end of the driveway and run.

Mom looks at me like I'm a ghost. She didn't expect me back in the house. "What?" she says. "I can hear the bus."

"String," I say. "I need string."

"For school?" she says.

"For . . . science. Actually, for a squirrel."

"A squirrel! You don't mess with squirrels," she says. "They can carry rabies."

"Not this one," I say, but it scares me, thinking about how it tried to bite Jake. "Can I take some string?"

She pulls a ball of it from the junk drawer, hands it to me, and I'm gone.

"Don't bang the door," she yells.

School bus brakes always squeal. Always. Jake's still in the road by the squirrel, and the bus has to squeal to a stop before it gets to the driveway, so it won't flatten either of them. Jake's not budging.

The school bus door folds open like hungry lips.

"Jake, what are we gonna do?" I ask.

"You helpin' me or not?" Jake asks.

"How we gonna get to school?"

Jake shrugs. "Don't you think this is more important than school?"

"You kids coming?" the bus driver yells.

I look at the bus, and I can see all the kids smashing their noses along the windows on our side of the bus, staring at us. "I'll miss my spelling test," I say.

"Jesus." Jake stands up to face me. I've never seen him look this angry. "Jesus," he says again. "Go take your friggin' spelling test."

I throw Jake the ball of string and grab my backpack. I see the little squirrel, and he's so scared I can see his heart pounding through his fur. I step onto the bus.

The bus driver is holding the door lever, ready to slam it shut behind me and swallow me into the mob. "Jake coming?" he asks.

I shake my head no.

The bus driver slams the door behind me. "What a loser," he says, shaking his head and jamming the bus into first. He has to back up a few feet to get around Jake and the squirrel.

"Wait!" I scream. I'm down the steps, leaning on the bus door. "Let me off."

The bus burps me out. "Suit yourself," the bus driver yells at my back. "Not my responsibility."

The bus roars away, and I have a sinking feeling in my gut.

Jake grins at me. "You're okay," he says.

I should have stayed on the bus.

Jake takes off his jacket and throws it over the squirrel, who fights and scratches like crazy so that Jake can't grab hold of it himself. His jacket is getting bloody, and Mom just washed it in the load of clothes she did for him. Jake finally gets it around the squirrel and pulls. When the smashed leg comes loose from the pavement, the squirrel turns into a little tornado of teeth and claws, but Jake drags him off the road and into the driveway, leaving a thin bloody trail.

Jake slips the jacket up so it's just over the squirrel's top half, exposing what's left of the back legs and tail. The squirrel squirms right out and snaps at Jake's hand again. This time he gets a little chunk of skin, and Jake yelps and jumps back. The squirrel writhes on the ground, but he can't get away.

Everybody's bleeding but me.

"Jake, what if he's got rabies?"

"He doesn't have rabies." Jake sounds disgusted. "He's not attacking 'cause he's vicious. He's just scared to death."

I wish I'd stayed on the bus.

Jake manages to slip the messy jacket back around the squirrel's head and front legs. "Here," he says, "hold him." Jake peels out the string and starts to wrap it around the squirrel's thigh, but the good back leg kicks it away and scratches Jake's hand. Now he has three little bloody lines down the back of his hand plus a small chunk of flesh gone by his first knuckle. He pulls off the jacket and starts over, covering everything but the mangled leg and the tail. Then he wraps the string again and pulls it tight. "Hold him down," he says.

The coat jerks and flops like a fish on a hook. I push down so hard I think I'm probably suffocating the poor thing, but I just keep pushing.

Jake wraps the string high around the thigh, just above the mangled part. I want to look away, but I can't. He pulls it tight, and the squirrel kicks and screams inside the jacket. Then he pulls the string tighter, and the squirrel jerks like the life is going out of him. Jake hangs on tight to the string, and I push hard on the edges of the jacket. I hear a little rip. I think the squirrel is biting right through the nylon.

"Jake," I say.

"It'll work," he says.

He pulls the string even tighter while he ties it. The thigh is the fattest part of the squirrel's leg, but Jake has squeezed it so tight that it's not much bigger around than the bone sticking out below.

"I think I'm ready to operate," he says. He pulls out his pocketknife and tests three blades against his thumb. The squirrel squirms, hard. Jake's own blood is making a little rivulet down his wrist.

I push down as hard as I can. "Please hurry," I say. "I don't know how long I can hold him."

"Hold on," he says.

He puts a knife to the bloody fur just above the main elbowlike joint. The knife slips through the muscle easily, like cutting meat, and my ears and teeth feel the grain of the muscle, like when we butcher chickens. I turn my face away.

Jake hits bone and starts sawing. The squirrel goes crazy, fighting for its life.

Jake has to drop the knife to help me hold. He reaches

under my arm in such a way that his upper arm touches my breast, but he doesn't even pay attention. Finally the squirrel settles down a little, getting exhausted, and Jake starts sawing again. I hold on with every ounce of strength I've got.

Cutting through chicken bones is nothing compared to this. Jake has to stop three more times to help me hold. Finally, finally, he's through it.

I relax, and the instant I do, the squirrel slips out of the jacket, thrashing and biting. We both jump back. He hisses at us and grabs for the string around his thigh with his teeth. He can't get it off, so he flips over and tries to run. He falls like a truck without a back wheel. He whips around to bite at the missing leg and screams again. Then he balances on three legs and hops-drags himself to the first apple tree on the edge of the orchard, tries to go up, falls, and sits in a ball at the bottom, looking at us and shaking.

"Give him space," Jake says. We back up a couple steps. The squirrel eyes us until he seems to think we're going to stay where we are, then he pulls himself up the tree, about as fast as a two-year-old could climb the ladder into the haymow.

I look at Jake. He grins at me and shrugs.

"Look at your jacket," I say.

Jake bends over, trying not to make any sudden movements. The squirrel is in the lowest crotch of the tree, still shaking and watching us. Jake lifts his jacket and the squirrel screams at him. Jake stops, picks up something else, and turns toward me, dangling the mashed, amputated leg. "Want this?" he asks.

"You're sick!" I say and whirl away from him, toward the house. On the way to the house, I see the blood splattered across the front of my brand-new T-shirt.

The screen door bangs shut ahead of us. Mom is on the porch, hands on her hips. Her soft curly hair looks grayer than usual in the sunshine. She's small with a round tummy. She's usually not a scary person, but now she's quiet, and her eyes are more terrible than any words.

"Mom, you let the door slam," I say.

Mom doesn't smile.

Jake stands, holding his knife and his blood-smeared jacket. His hair hangs over one eye, and there are spatters of blood on his baby-face cheeks. His jacket is a mess and he wipes his knife on his sleeve. He looks down, but he's not ashamed.

Most mothers would probably faint if they saw all the blood on us, but my mom is only angry.

We tell her what we did, making it sound very noble, but she just tells Jake he'll have to have rabies shots in the belly. "Unless you can catch the squirrel again," she says, "and kill it. So they can test it for rabies."

"Mom, we just saved its life. We're not killing it," I say.

"You'd rather have Jake die of rabies?" she asks.

I look at Jake and then at the ground. Not right now. A couple days ago, yes, but not right now. I don't answer her.

After we've both had showers and put on clean clothes, Mom hydrogen peroxides Jake's squirrel bite and scratches for fifteen minutes until they quit fizzing, bandages his hand, and drives us to school in the truck. I have to sit in the middle.

I'm really mad about the blood on my new Cubs shirt, but I don't say anything about it. I left it soaking in cold water in the bathroom sink.

On the way to school, Jake says, "Maybe I should be a vet."

"Maybe you should," Mom says.

"Yeah, right," I say. "Vets go to college for about eight years."

Jake just looks out the passenger's window.

CHAPTER 6

Mom won't sign excuses for us, so we have to wait to talk to the principal before we can get passes into our second-period classes. I hate sitting in the office with Jake.

Meredith Baker, wearing a very tight leather miniskirt, swishes in to deliver the attendance sheet from second-period English. I can't help noticing that she managed to get the paint out of her hair. I try to smile at her, but Jake is staring at her skirt, and when she sees him looking, she looks away from both of us as if looking might contaminate her.

Finally, the secretary comes out of the principal's inner office and tells Jake to go in. "Come with me," she says to me. I get up and follow her down a short hall to the door of the counselor's office. "Sit right here," she says, indicating a chair in the hall.

I sit. I feel like a grade-school kid in trouble, swinging her feet while she waits on a chair outside the principal's office. I'm glad that at least my feet touch the floor.

The door opens and the counselor floats out of her office in a cloud of flowery perfume, anchored to the ground by the clacking of her high heels and the weight of her hips. I've tried wearing perfume, and it gives me a headache every time. I feel a headache coming on as soon as I smell Mrs. Prebyl. She's wearing a peachy-pink dress that clings, with a belt to match. The belt buckle is sort of antique gold and her earrings are the same kind of color, with an inch-wide peachy-pink pearl in the middle. Even her shoes are peachy-pink and so is the blush on her cheeks. I can't tell if she's old enough to have wrinkles, or if her make up is so thick that it cracks in the corners of her eyes when she makes herself smile at me. Her hair is a solid auburn, without a hint of any other color; it must be dyed. I still don't have a clue how old she is.

I don't trust anybody who looks like that.

"So, how are we today, Elaine?" she asks, smiling so hard that I think some chunks of makeup will fall off, but they don't.

"Fine." I swallow the words I want to say. *We? How*

are we? And I hate being called Elaine.

"What happened this morning, Elaine? Why were you late?"

I look at my hands in my lap.

"I must know before I can write a pass for you into your second-hour class. That's all. Now just tell me what happened . . ."

"I had something I needed to do."

"But your parents didn't give you permission. No one wrote an excuse, so they must not have found it so necessary." Now I can hear the anger in her voice, all the judgment that she's hiding behind the makeup mask.

"No. Mom thought I was on my way to school, until we came into the house and the bus had gone. And I was going to school. I really was. I even got on the bus."

"We? Elaine, do you mean you and Jake Riley?"

"Call me Lainey."

"Okay, Lainey, when you say 'we,' do you mean you and Jake?"

"Yes."

"What was it that was so important? You've never been so late before without a note. It's not like you. And good students like you don't just skip class."

I can hear Dad saying that if I let Jake talk me into something, it's my fault.

"There was a squirrel. Jim Pietzman hit it with his car, and it was lying in the road, screaming, and Jake and I had to do something. We couldn't just leave it there. I thought we should shoot it . . . but Jake thought we could save it." I look her in the eye. "It wasn't irreparably damaged."

It takes a moment for this to register with Mrs. Prebyl. When she realizes that I'm referring to her file on Jake, her face goes scarlet, with chalky white lines around her nose. I watch her face, amazed that so much color can show through all the paint she wears. She swallows, straightens her peachy back, and asks, her voice almost shaking with anger, "Elaine, are you romantically involved with Jake?"

"No way!" The words sort of splatter out. I see a teeny drop of saliva fly in the direction of Mrs. Prebyl's lap. Another wave of discomfort circulates beneath her makeup. She makes a brushing motion toward her peachy-pink skirt where my saliva would have landed. I would be mortified if I didn't feel so much like spitting at her. "But I don't think that's any of your business, anyhow."

"If you're not romantically involved, then why do you protect him, Elaine?"

"Call me Lainey. I don't, when he's wrong," I say.

She looks at me.

"This morning, I'm sure he was right. Obviously, Mom disagreed. But then she sticks up for him when I hate him."

She sighs, as if she can breathe the topic of Jake out of her system. "So, what did you and Jake Riley do?" she asks. Her words sound like she's trying to step daintily over a mud puddle.

"With the squirrel?"

She nods.

"Jake said we could amputate its leg like they did in Civil War hospitals. The squirrel couldn't move, 'cause his hind leg was plastered to the pavement. Jake tied off the leg with a piece of string and cut it off." I think of Jake's pocketknife. Now I've sort of told that he has a knife, so I finish, "I went into the house to get the stuff to do it, and Mom told me to stay away from squirrels."

"But you did it anyway."

I nod. "It seemed like the right thing to do. Humane or something."

I can't read Mrs. Prebyl's face very well. I'm expecting her to start on a tirade about how we could have gotten rabies, and if I tell her that the squirrel broke Jake's skin, she'll probably make him take rabies shots in the stomach, so I don't say any more.

"Can I go to class now? That's all that happened. After we let the squirrel go, I mean."

She clears her throat, as if it would force her face back to normal. "The principal," she says, "wanted me to talk to you because we're concerned about your involvement with Jake. The bus driver reported that you got off the bus to be with him. Such behavior seems to be uncharacteristic for you."

I feel myself go limp like a noodle, and deep red creeps over my own face. I think of what Jake has tried, that they can't possibly know. "My involvement?"

"Well, your . . . friendship."

I stare at her. What do they think? Why are they talking about Jake and me in the principal's office?

She waits for me to say something, but I just keep staring at her.

"Elaine, I'm concerned . . ."

"Lainey."

"Lainey, I'm concerned—we're concerned—that Jake was able to talk you into doing something like this so that you end up shirking your primary responsibility, which is school. It's out of character, and we want to nip it in the bud, so to speak." I can hear Dad's voice again in my head. I try to concentrate on Mrs. Prebyl, because she can't be worse than Dad will be tonight. "And you yourself said that you hate him sometimes."

"Well, yeah, he does some real stupid things, and sometimes I hate him. But sometimes he's real good, too. If something or someone is dying, don't you stop and help?" I ask.

"That's different."

"How's it different? What if the superintendent called you to a meeting about your job and, on the way to his office, one of us was bleeding on the sidewalk. You'd leave us?"

"Of course not, Elaine. Don't be silly."

"*Lainey*. I'm not being silly. You're supposed to help us. At home, I take care of animals. That's one of my jobs. This time, a squirrel needed help."

"But you're not responsible for squirrels."

"Oh, so if it were a kid from North Polk High bleeding to death, you'd leave him, 'cause you're not responsible for him?"

"Elaine." Her voice is fierce now, so I don't correct her this time, and I guess it's time to stop arguing. "What's important here, Elaine, is the fact that *Jake* has the kind of influence over you that could keep you from your responsibilities. That's why we're concerned about your involvement. You're very bright. You understand that."

"It was the squirrel . . ."

"I was informed that only when the bus driver insulted Jake did you jump off the bus, as if you have some sort of allegiance to him."

I feel sick. I'm wasting my breath. "Can I go to class now?"

"Yes." She picks up a hall pass and fills it out. She holds it toward me, and I stand up to take it, but she doesn't let go until she says, "Think about why you really stayed with Jake. Don't let someone like that spoil your chances for real success in this world, Elaine."

Someone like that, she says. "What about Jake?" My voice is louder than I expected. "He's one of your students, too. He's *not* my boyfriend, but he might be a good veterinarian."

Her laughing face reminds me of a peachy-pink Wicked Witch of the West. "Jake? He'll have to turn over a new leaf if he wants to go to college at all, much less veterinary school."

I pull the pass away and turn to leave. I hate it that Mrs. Prebyl has the same reaction that I did to the idea of Jake becoming a vet. I'm in such a hurry to get out of there, I bang my foot against her door. It hurts while I walk down the hall.

CHAPTER 7

Mr. Reed ignores me when I hand him the pass and slip into my spot at the art table. Jailene looks at me as if I have grown scales. I stare at my books on the table. Mr. Reed spends the whole period lecturing about the color wheel, so Jailene doesn't get a chance to say anything until we're on our way out the door.

"You skipped school with *Jake* this morning? I thought you didn't like him! Everybody's talking about you guys. How come you didn't tell me?"

"There's nothing to tell!" I turn on her and she backs off, bumping into the nearest locker. "We just helped a stupid squirrel that got hit in the road." I think about telling her about the blood and my new Cubs shirt, but I hold off.

"Holy buckets, Lainey, don't get so pissed off at me. I just wanted to know."

"Sorry. It's just . . . I can't believe it. Even Mrs.

Prebyl asked me if I'm *romantically involved* with Jake."

"Are you?"

"Jeez, Jailene!"

"I'm kidding. But Prebyl asked you that? That's none of her business, is it?"

"Would I kid about anything so idiotic?"

We wedge our way down the hall until we meet Amy. When we pass a bunch of freshmen lockers, I get whistled at. Somebody hoots, "Ooh, baby, Lainey just got laid," and everybody laughs. Amy looks at me, trying not to giggle. "What are they talking about?"

"Shut *up*!" I yell toward the lockers and hurry down the hall, leaving Amy and Jailene staring after me. I know I should have ignored those boys, and that saying something back to them was the worst thing I could do, but it just came out.

I run toward the American studies room. I turn the corner too fast and slam—full-body contact—into Arcadia Knowles.

"Whoa," she says.

"I'm sorry, I'm so sorry, I . . ."

She frowns at me, but it's not an unfriendly look. "Watch it," she says, with the corners of her mouth twisting up.

"I really am sorry." I step around her.

"Let me guess," Arcadia says. "You missed first period and you're still running to catch up with the day."

My feet stop moving and I feel my jaw hanging open, stupidly, as I turn back toward her. "You noticed?"

"What? That you weren't in English? Hard to miss. You're the only interesting person in the room." She grins. "See you later." She begins to walk down the hall then turns. "Oh, hey, what's your name?"

"Lainey."

"Hope you catch up, Lainey." She melts into the crowded hall, leaving me standing there with a mouth like a fish.

She got it wrong. She's definitely more interesting than I am. I'm just me, but she's probably one of the most interesting people in the whole school, for that matter.

That night, I finish my homework at the kitchen table without saying a word. Mom doesn't talk to me, either. I clear off my homework, set the table, and help dish up the baked chicken, mashed potatoes, gravy, and corn.

Dad comes in and I don't look at him. We all focus on the food as if it's the most important thing in the world. Little golden nuggets grown from our own soil that pop between our teeth, potatoes all fleshy and white that were covered with our own black dirt just a few weeks ago. We let the food consume us so we don't have to talk, and I wonder what it would be like to have a sister or a brother, so all this energy wouldn't have to zero in on me.

Dad sets his fork down after he finishes his first helping of chicken and runs his hand through his hair. "Lainey." His hair is straight and thick, so light brown that the gray parts don't show much. Now there are furrows in it where his fingers went.

"Yes." I wipe my mouth and let my hands lie on top of the napkin in my lap in case they shake.

"Your mother says you were late for school this morning because you were messing around with Jake."

"Messing around?" I look to Mom for help, but she gets up to refill the gravy boat. "I wasn't 'messing around.'"

Dad shrugs it off. "You know what I mean. Goofing around."

"Dad, there was a squirrel in the road, and we saved its life. Is that messing around?"

"Lainey, your job right now is to get a good education so you can contribute back to the world, so you can *be* something."

I'm not anything now, I guess.

"Squirrels carry rabies, and they steal our grain. A dead squirrel is no great loss to the countryside. It happens."

"I know that, Dad. But it was suffering. It was just so helpless."

"You should have just put it out of its misery, Lainey. It'll die anyway, without a leg and bleeding like that. Lots of things are helpless. Think about the baby pigs we lose. Some things are worth fighting for and some aren't. Guess you need to learn that. We can't do everything in this life, so we have to choose where to put our energy.

"I'm going over to Granger tomorrow. They've got a load of baby calves to sell. I mean *baby* calves. Had to get them away from their mamas quick, 'cause there was a rash of mastitis. And these little guys are still suckin'."

I feel myself light up. Baby calves are cute and fuzzy. Of course, they grow into cattle, but they're all snuggly with soft faces and necks when they're little.

"I'm gonna buy a few and get a couple nursing buckets while I'm out."

I smile, but I'm afraid to hope, almost afraid that, for punishment, Dad won't let me help with the calves.

"They're gonna be yours, Lainey. *All* yours. Give you some responsibility. Some sense of what life is worth savin'. What money's worth and what time's worth. How much it takes to raise something that's worth some money."

Mom's looking uncomfortable.

"You can feed them every morning before school to keep you from thinking you got time to mess around with squirrels, and you can feed them at night and keep their pen clean. It's all up to you. I'll buy the feed—at first that'll be mostly calf formula—and I'll feed them at noon if they're still little enough to need it, at least until we start combining, but I'm not doing anything else. They will be dependent on you. Your babies, Lainey."

I feel a knot in my stomach. I want them badly—I want to touch their little noses and feel their sandpapery tongues and fuzzy heads—but this will be lots and lots of work. And Dad has never made me chore in the mornings before.

The next day, I wake up forty-five minutes early and go for a run. I should get back into running every day, so that by spring I'll be deadly for the distance track team. I won't have time in the mornings for a while, with baby calves to feed.

We live one-third of a mile from one corner and two-thirds from the other. Everything here on this flat Iowa farmland is divided off in perfect one-mile square sections. I got Dad to watch the odometer with me so I know that it's exactly one mile to the Hatchers' mailbox in the next section past Jake's house, and a mile from our driveway to a certain telephone pole beyond a fence the other way. The half miles have landmarks, too. That way I have all sorts of distances up to four miles around the section marked off for running.

This morning I run two. To Hatchers' mailbox and back. I jog easy at first, then I push harder, touch their mailbox, run as fast as I can back to our driveway, then jog up the driveway. According to the clock on the microwave, it only took me fourteen minutes and fifty-two seconds, counting the jogging. Not bad.

I shower, have breakfast, and wait until the last minute to go out to the end of the driveway to wait for the bus, which is just pulling to a stop to pick up Jake at his driveway.

People at school give a few catcalls, and I avoid the hallway where I embarrassed myself yesterday. Before English, I see Mrs. Prebyl coming down the hall, so I turn my back and concentrate on my locker combination.

I'm the first one to sit down in English, and I bury my nose in *To Kill a Mockingbird* before anybody else walks in. I finish the book in our eight reading minutes. Actually, I finish it in the first five. I was almost done in bed last night, but I didn't dare leave my light on a minute past ten-thirty when dad was so mad at me already.

I don't want the book to be over. I'll miss spending time with Scout every day. Being done is like losing a friend. Then you have to start over and make new ones in a new book.

The father in this book, Atticus Finch, says that most people are "real nice . . . when you finally see them."

I run my finger up and down the cellophane library book jacket, and I think of Jake. I know he has niceness inside. I've seen it, not all that often of course, but I wonder if it could come out at school if teachers would let it. It's pretty hard to see when he can be so obnoxious. And what about the boys at Eldora? Was there anything nice about them, even with what they did to Jake? Maybe. Or maybe Atticus Finch was wrong, and there are just evil, mean people in the world who can't let any niceness out.

Finally, I set the book down and look around the room. Arcadia Knowles is reading a novel instead of her

Muscle & Fitness magazine. She's intent on the story and starts shaking with silent laughter. Then she looks up, grinning, and sees me watching at her. I'm embarrassed that she caught me looking, but she just covers her mouth, rolls her eyes, and goes back to the story. I can't figure her out.

Then reading time is over and I have to think about irregular verbs. Eikton throws grammar in between creative writing sessions so we won't hate it so much.

At the end of the hour, Eikton hands back our haikus, and he has written, *Please see me, Elaine. You have a writing talent. Keep up the good work.* I feel a little lighter inside, and when the bell rings I wait for the classroom to empty.

"Elaine," he says, "you had some wonderful images in your poetry." He smiles at me.

I smile back. "Thanks." There's something coming, though. I can see from his smile that he didn't ask me to wait after class just to compliment me.

"I've selected ten of the best haiku from the class, and I'd like to read them to everyone tomorrow."

Panic hits me and crawls from my stomach to my neck.

"All of your poems are in the ten, but I wanted to

check with you before I read them."

"No!" I feel a drip of cold sweat under each armpit.

"Don't worry, that's why I'm asking. I bet you don't want me to read the one about Jake. Am I right?"

I nod.

"I figured as much. Actually, I wouldn't read something like that without asking. But do I have your permission to read the others? They're very good, especially the one about the combine."

"Thanks, yeah. Okay." I feel myself blushing. "Can you call me Lainey? I hate Elaine."

"Sure." He grins.

I grasp for something else to say. "Can I take my spelling test today? The one I missed yesterday?"

"Anytime. I heard about the squirrel."

"You did?"

He nods. "Mrs. Prebyl told me."

"Guess the whole school knows. So much for counselors and confidentiality."

Mr. Eikton frowns.

"Can I take the spelling test seventh period?"

"Fine. See you then."

I move toward the door.

"Lainey?" he says.

"Yeah?"

"Is everything okay? I mean, I thought saving the squirrel was noble."

"Really?"

He nods. "Risky, but noble."

I wait. I can tell he wants to say something else. I'm not sure I want to hear it or not, but I guess I'd better stay and find out.

"What's Jake like? I mean, between the poem you wrote about him and saving the squirrel, he sounds a bit . . . complicated."

"A *bit*! Ha. Jake is *just* my neighbor. Everybody's making this big deal out of it. He drives me nuts, but since he lives next door, Mom makes me be nice to him. Then he does something like saving the squirrel, so I think he's okay. But he doesn't have any other friends and he's always around, so most of the time I just feel stuck with him. That's *all*."

"That's what the poem meant?"

I shrug. And nod.

"I need to tell you something."

Panic rises again.

"I showed off some of your poems in the lounge this morning. Sometimes we do that when a student's work amazes us. And your talent is impressive. But after what you just said about Mrs. Prebyl, I'm sorry I did it. I just meant to compliment you."

"Did Prebyl see them?"

Mr. Eikton nods. "I'm really sorry. I had no idea it was any big deal. I just figured Jake was a boyfriend or an irritating friend or something. Then she told me about the squirrel and that she's very concerned about your involvement with Jake."

I feel my face fire up. "I can't *believe* you showed her that poem. You're the only teacher I trusted. *Prebyl*, of all people."

There are second-period students filing into the room now. I turn on my heel to leave.

"Wait, Lainey," he says. "Can I do something to help?"

"You've done too much, I think," I say.

"Lainey, keep writing," he says. The words bounce off my back as I'm headed out the door.

The noises of the hall close in on me. I don't hear Jailene yelling down the hall, "Lainey, wait!" She finally catches me as we slide into our spots for art. "What is wrong with you? You deaf or something? Some friend you are lately."

"Sorry," I say, trying to look apologetic with my eyebrows.

She rolls her eyes. "Peter Stortman asked me to go with him to homecoming."

"So are you going out with him?"

"Yeah, diphead. You've been too busy with Jake to pay attention."

"Shut up!"

She ignores me. "Well, I'm not *going with him*, but we have a date Saturday night."

"Wow. Peter Stortman. Don't get him near any paint cans, okay?"

Jailene starts giggling. "He's so funny. So crazy."

"Sounds like a barrel of laughs to me. I did notice yesterday that Meredith got the paint out of her hair."

Jailene rolls her eyes. "Meredith deserved it, from what I heard."

"So are you going? To homecoming with him, I mean?"

"Of course. Think you'll go with Jake?"

"Are you nuts? Of course not. He's *not* my *boyfriend*. I can barely stand him as a friend."

"Right."

Jailene's teasing, but I'm not. She tries to read my face. "What?" she asks.

"Nothing."

"Tell me."

"Nothing," I say. "Just that something about Peter makes me nervous for you. I don't know what it is."

"Well, something about Jake makes me nervous!"

"Yeah, you and me both. And the rest of the world, for that matter. But *you and Peter* and *Jake and I* are not the same thing. I'm not *going out* with Jake. You *are* going out with Peter."

"So what's wrong with Peter?"

"I just think he can be a jerk."

Jailene scowls at me and *humph*s to her side of the table.

"So, don't ask me, if you don't want my opinion. I'm glad for you if you're happy," I say.

Mr. Reed is starting to take attendance.

"At least Peter's not a butcher veterinarian with greasy hair!" Jailene hisses at me in whisper.

"Shut up." Why does it always have to be like this, if you want somebody's friendship? Say exactly the right thing or you risk losing your friend. I think if I don't watch it, I'll wind up without a friend in the world.

"Jailene," I whisper underneath Mr. Reed's voice, "I'm sorry. Maybe I'm jealous that you've got a real date." Fat chance. Well, maybe I am. I do wonder what it would be like.

Jailene shrugs and grins at me. "'S'okay."

We're doing papier-mâché animals and it feels good to get my hands slimy and sticky, fitting newspaper strips around the wire frame of my calf. I wish I had done an owl or cat sitting, so I didn't have four legs to plaster. I should have at least made him lying down. I also wonder if I'll be sick of looking at calves long before I get my plaster one done.

Amy joins us in the hall since we have third period together. I make them go the long way around to avoid that certain string of lockers. Later we inch through the lunch line together, waiting for footlongs, green beans, applesauce, and chocolate chip cookies. The cookie is hardly worth the wait.

Amy wants a date for homecoming in the worst way. I tell her there's plenty of time to get one, but she wants to go with me if neither of us has one by then.

"That's the last thing I'm worried about right now, Ame," I say, squirting parallel lines of ketchup and mustard down my dog.

"How can you not worry about a date for homecoming?"

"Dad's really mad at me for skipping the beginning of school yesterday, and he's buying calves today."

"Calves? Like baby cows? So?"

"For me. I have to do everything for them. He says it'll make me understand what real responsibility is. For lives that are 'worthwhile' instead of something useless like a squirrel."

"Makes sense to me," Amy says. She shudders. "I can't believe you helped Jake saw off a live squirrel's leg."

I shrug. While we eat, Jailene runs through a list of what she might wear on her date Saturday night. Neither of us are any help because Peter hasn't told Jailene where they're going.

Licking the last crumb of cookie from my finger, I say, "I need a new library book, so, since we've still got ten minutes, I'm gonna go to the library. Anybody want to come with me?"

They shake their heads, and Amy makes a face. She hates to read, and English class is a chore for her. At eight minutes a day, she'll be lucky to finish one book all semester, especially since all she seems to read is *Sassy* magazine. I don't understand anybody who doesn't like to read.

"See ya."

"Bye. See ya in Spanish," says Amy.

I've dumped my tray and I'm almost out the door when Jake walks in. What timing. He doesn't even have lunch now.

"Why, Lainey-Belainey! Assistant to the veterinarian."

"Shut up, Jake."

I hear Jailene behind me saying, "Look!" and I feel my ears go red.

Jake steps in my path so I can't get out.

"Just let me by, Jake," I say.

"What? I'm not good enough for you now?"

"Look, I'm taking enough crap for this. Please. I just want to get to the library before class."

"I'll escort you."

"No! I don't want or need a blasted escort. Now leave me alone!" I shove past him, but he jumps after me and grabs my arm so he won't be embarrassed, being bested by a girl in front of the whole lunchroom. "Let go of me, Jake. Right now." Jake holds on tight.

I hear the sudden silence in the lunchroom behind me, and when I turn to see the reason for the quiet, I look up into Mrs. Prebyl's face.

Jake drops my arm in a split second.

"Is there a problem here?" Those words could be an invitation to help with a problem, but the way she says them is not. Her voice has cold, sharp edges. She's not peachy-pink today. She's black-and-white like her voice; her skirt is properly flared over her wide hips, and her shirtwaist blouse is crisp with a black-and-white cameo brooch at the neck and earrings to match.

"No problem," Jake says, looking at his toes. "See ya, Lainey-Bel—"

"I think you'd both better come with me," Mrs. Prebyl says, crisp as her blouse.

"I'm on my way to the library. Please, Mrs. Prebyl. I only have a few minutes before my next class."

"Elaine, Jake, you're both coming with me."

"Nothing's wrong, ma'am," Jake says, seeing the anger in my face. "I was just being a dink, and I wanted Lainey to stay here and talk to me. She's not a problem."

I stare at him, admiring him for this.

"It's my fault," he says. "She just wants to go to the library."

Mrs. Prebyl stops, confused.

Jake says, "It's not her fault. Let her go."

Mrs. Prebyl's eyebrows go up so far that her makeup threatens to crack in lines on her forehead.

"Well, then," she tries to regain her composure. "When do the two of you have study hall so we can straighten this out?"

"I swear, there's nothing to straighten out," Jake says.

Her black-and-white look doesn't soften, so I say, "Seventh period."

"I'll send a pass. Jake?"

"My dad's picking me up in half an hour. I have to go talk to the doctor to see if I need a rabies shot. That's what I was trying to tell Lainey when you showed up."

During sixth-period Spanish, I can't take my mind off rabies shots and Mrs. Prebyl whose world is black-and-white. I want the time to drag, so I don't have to go see Prebyl, but it speeds by too fast.

At 2:04, I get the pass from Mr. Hinson and head toward my fate. At first, it seems as if it won't be so bad. All she asks is more about our minor skirmish in the lunchroom today. But then she pulls her chair up to her desk, puts her elbows on the desktop, and folds her hands under her chin. "Elaine. I read some of your poetry this morning."

That reminds me. "Oh, my gosh! I forgot. I was supposed to take Mr. Eikton's spelling test this period."

"You'll still have time when we're through here, Elaine."

"Lainey. Please."

She looks at me as if I've asked her to cut the leg off a squirrel. "Now then, what I need to say is that I have cause for real concern. What has Jake Riley been trying to do? You don't write about running and getting away from someone whom you consider a real friend unless something is going on. Then I find him holding you against your will at the lunchroom doorway. What is it, Elaine?"

"It's Lainey. Please don't call me Elaine." My armpits start sweating. I wonder exactly what she said to Eikton this morning. For a moment, I think it would be a relief to tell her that Jake threatened me with his rifle, but I think about the pleasure she'd get from proving her theory that he's "irreparably damaged." I can only imagine she'd ship him right back to the school in Eldora if I told her, so I say, "Nothing. He's my neighbor. He can be very irritating, but that's *it*. That's *all*."

She sighs. "I can't help you or Jake, Elaine, if you don't talk to me."

I want to tell her we don't need help, but I'm sure it would just infuriate her. Plus, I'm not sure it's entirely true that I don't need help, and I think Jake *does* need help. We just don't need it from her. So I don't say anything until she finally lets me go take my spelling test.

On the school bus home, I wedge myself between a seventh-grade girl and the window, jump off the bus as soon as it stops, and run to the house.

I can hear baby calves bawling.

CHAPTER 8

Mom grins at me when I plop my book bag by the door. I remember not to let it bang shut.

"They're real cute," she says.

I start for the barn.

"Nuh-uh. Change your clothes first."

I run upstairs to put on old clothes, then I bolt out the door. In the barn, I see Dad is in the pen with them. There are four calves. Every one is different: red-and-white like a Hereford, black-and-white like a dairy Holstein, almost-white like a Charolais, and tawny red-brown like a shorthorn.

"It was a mixed-up bunch. Holstein bull got loose in this guy's beef heifers. Hard to believe he got this hodge-podge. I talked to the guy before the sale. Said he just buys up whatever young heifers or steers he can get, 'cause he's got a hundred acres of pasture and isn't set up to milk enough Holsteins to make use of all his land.

'These calves are a waste of good Holstein seed,' the guy said." Dad grins at me.

I climb into the pen with them.

Dad watches me for a minute, then goes on. "A whole lot of this guy's cows got mastitis, and he didn't have time to mess with the calves. I got there early, so I sort of had my pick. Thought you'd like them all different. All good calves."

"Wow." I'm squatting in the pen so I don't look intimidating to the little guys. "Thanks, Dad."

Dad is fastening a calf-high feeder to the side of the bunk because the bunk is too high for their little noses to reach. These calves look really young, barely a week old. I reach out my hand to them, and they back up to the corner, but it makes them go closer to Dad, and they don't know who they should fear the most.

"Cute little geezers, aren't they?"

"Yeah, they sure are."

He takes off his green Pioneer cap by the bill, scratches the top of his head with the same hand, and grins at me. "You should have heard the ruckus in the sale barn with fifty of these little critters bawling for their mamas."

"Poor babies."

Dad motions to the white plastic water trough that's

in the bunk. "Gotta put that up next, then we'll mix up their formula so you'll know how you're gonna be doing this. You're their new mama."

I hold the little trough while he wires and sets it. Then he sends me to the house for four gallons of warm water. We mix the formula in a bucket: three scoops of mix to a gallon of water. It looks like dark powdered milk and smells like baby formula. Dad produces two two-gallon buckets that have rubber nipples, bigger than Dad's thumb, attached at the bottom corner. We slosh half of the formula in each bucket and then we balance them on the edge of the bunk where the calves can grab on if they stretch their necks upward.

They stare at us, eyes wide and empty.

"Don't they know what they're supposed to do?"

Dad shakes his head. "We'll have to show them. They were just weaned. Their first meal on the bucket is right here."

Dad sets one bucket down inside the bunk. "Keep yours where it is, Lainey." He walks to the little red-and-white one and grabs him around the neck.

"Herby."

"What?" Dad asks.

"Herby. His name is Herby."

"Oh. Great. Well, Herby, you won't be needin' your

name if you don't eat something." He practically carries Herby over to me and the bucket. "You get his mouth on it," he says to me. "He'll suck like crazy, if you can just get it to his mouth."

I take Herby's little muzzle under the chin and pull it up to the level of the nipple. Herby shakes his head free from my fingers. Dad stands there, holding Herby where he is. I rub his head over the ears, and he jerks his head away from my touch. I pull his head up toward the bucket again, and he jumps, front feet off the ground in spite of the hold Dad's got on him.

"Get a clue, Herby," I say. I lift the bucket off the edge of the bunk, and Herby backs against Dad and wedges himself between Dad's legs. The other three are watching, wild-eyed, from the far corner of the pen.

I bring the bucket nipple closer to Herby's nose. He jerks his head just as Dad says, "Careful!" It catches me off guard and a good quart of formula sloshes out.

"See if you can get him to suck on your finger first," Dad says. "Then if he gets the action going, he'll transfer to the bucket." So I hold my finger out to his soft, whiskery mouth, and he lips it, then immediately he's sucking hard. It tickles, and it feels slimy, but it feels wonderful, too. He sucks really hard, like he means business. Dad grins at me and I grin back. "Now," he says.

I lead him a couple steps by my finger, Herby following his sucking instinct, with Dad right behind, and I rest the bucket on the edge of the bunk again. I pull his mouth to the nipple with my finger, then I slide the tip of the bucket nipple into the edge of his mouth and squeeze so a little milk squirts out and dribbles along my finger into his mouth. Herby swallows and quivers all over, as if he's starving. He doesn't want to let my finger go, but I pull it out with the sound of a very wet vacuum, and shove his mouth onto the nipple. He's sucking like crazy in a split second.

"Ha! We did it!" Herby jumps back because I'm too loud, and the milk bucket goes with him. I'm not holding it tight enough, and it flips right on top of him. All the formula runs down his little white face and dark red neck. He lets out a bleat.

"Damn," Dad says.

"I'm sorry. I'm so sorry. I'm sooo sorry."

Dad lets out a very angry sigh, and Herby looks more like an overgrown rat than a calf. Dad lets him go and he tries to hide behind the other calves, but he's tasted food and even though he's terrified, he wants more. The tawny calf licks the side of his face, and the Holstein starts in, too. In almost no time, the tawny calf is sucking on poor little Herby's milky ear.

Dad looks at me. We can't help laughing, but I know he expects me to fix the situation. They're my calves and I blew it, so I pick up the other bucket with both hands, hold it tightly to my chest, and walk up to Herby. He backs up a few paces, but smells the formula, remembers the taste of it, and steps toward me. He noses the bucket, I help him find the nipple, and he grabs it and sucks and sucks. The other calves follow, licking the milk off his head and neck.

I wrap my arms around the bucket and hold it tight against my stomach. I can feel it pulse with the rhythm of his sucking. I wonder if nursing a baby feels this way.

"Herby's no dummy," Dad says.

I scratch Herby over his damp ears while he sucks. He lets go and looks at me, a little nervous, but he comes right back for more. His sides go in and out, and we can actually see his tummy getting rounder as he drinks.

"I think he's had about enough for one feeding," Dad says. "Don't want him to explode."

I try to pull the bucket away from him, but he's sucking too hard, and he won't let go.

"Gotta stop him, Lainey. These little guys will drink until they're sick." When I still can't get the bucket away, Dad says, "Stick your finger into his mouth, beside the nipple, to break the vacuum. Then pull the nipple out."

It works. "There you go," Dad says. "One down, three to go."

We feed the little tawny one next. He's in the mood to suck because he got some milk off Herby's ear. He's not quite as nervous as Herby was, and we get him going right away. While I feed him, Dad finds two gunny sacks, gets one wet, and rubs some of the stickiness out of Herby's coat, then tries to dry him. Before we know it, the bucket is empty. I go to the house and get two more gallons of warm water to replace what I dumped all over Herby.

We're trying to grab the Holstein or the Charolais and Dad says, "After a night or two, your problem is going to be keeping them from knocking you over to get to the bucket first. And you'll have to fight the other three off to feed one."

The black-and-white calf puts up quite a fight, but we only spill a few more sloshes of formula. The white-tan calf is so hungry by the time he gets the nipple that he can't stand still when he's drinking. His little tail goes crazy like a bottle brush in a blender. He jerks so hard on the nipple that he practically pulls the bucket out of my arms. I hang on tight—I learned something from

Herby—but the front of my sweatshirt is soaked by the time he's done.

When we're through, I have to clean out the wet straw where I dumped almost two gallons of formula and then make sure there is plenty of hay to snuggle down in for the night. I rub Herby again with clean straw to make sure he's pretty dry. By the time I leave, all four of them have collapsed in a fuzzy pile. It's been a big day for them.

I carry the buckets to the house and wash them in the basement with very hot water, especially the nipples, and set them to dry on an old clean towel so they're ready for the morning feeding. Dad says he'll help me again in the morning, but that will be the last time. He'll feed them at noon for a week or so, and then they can go to twice-a-day feedings. He says he's got too much fieldwork to do to mess around with baby calves, and besides, the calves are supposed to teach me responsibility. I feel like a mother.

CHAPTER 9

I have to get up at five-thirty to be sure I have enough time to feed my calves before school. These babies are exhausting. I also have to allow time to take a shower in case one of my youngsters spills another bucket of formula down my shirt. I don't relish the idea of walking the halls smelling like baby formula.

As I'm getting ready to go to the barn, Mom says that when I was a baby, I used to spit up my first feeding of the morning all over her every day. "I fed you first, then I took a shower and threw my nightgown in the wash. That's how every day started."

"I must have been a barrel of fun," I say as I slip into my denim chore jacket.

It's so cool this autumn morning that steam rises from the warm water in the buckets as I carry them to the barn. My damp fingers are cold. I'll have to start wearing gloves when I do this.

The calves are curled against one another in a corner of their pen. They look little and cozy, and I'm glad to be here with warmth for their tummies. I quietly mix the formula into the warm water, but all four little heads are up and looking at me by the time I'm ready to feed them. The black-and-white Holstein gets to his feet and ambles over first.

"Good morning, Flower," I say as he noses around for the nipple.

"Flower?" Dad asks from behind me. He's been getting bedding ready for the sows, and I didn't hear him come up beside the calf pen.

"Yeah, like Flower, the skunk in *Bambi*. You know, black-and-white."

Dad nods and grins. "So is the little fawn-colored guy named Bambi?"

"I haven't decided yet." Of course I'd thought of calling him Bambi, but I decided not to because it's too obvious and unoriginal. I think it's wise now, however, to give Dad some consideration in this situation. I look at Dad. "Um, yeah. Let's name him Bambi." Dad gives me a smile.

The feeding goes much easier this time. I have to pry each calf off the bucket so they all get their fair share. Dad helps me put some nutrition supplement into the automatic feeder that he put up in their pen yesterday. "In case they get really hungry between feedings and don't think they can wait for their milk, they can munch on this stuff a little bit."

There's powdered milk in the feed pellets—I can tell by the smell. When we wean them from the nipple buckets, we'll give them formula in troughs for a while; then, finally, this supplement will be their main food. We also fill their automatic watering trough, which I say should have a nipple. Dad says they'll start drinking from the trough easily enough. It's not worth the hassle of rigging up a trough with a nipple.

"We could just put water in a milk bucket and tie it here."

"Yeah, I suppose so." Dad takes off his cap and scratches his head. "But then they won't associate the nipple with milk, and they might not be such eager eaters at meals."

"Oh, okay."

"You're thinkin', though," Dad says.

I have time to help Dad throw bedding to the lambs before we go to the house for breakfast.

He grins at me, and it feels good.

Mom has pancakes and bacon waiting for us. I feel like I earned my keep this morning.

•   •   •

I wear my Cubs shirt (Mom got all the blood out) with a cardigan under my denim jacket, since I've had a good taste of how cool the morning is. Jake yells at me from his driveway and I wave and turn my back, hoping to discourage him from coming over.

I can hear his feet approaching. I wish the bus would come.

"Lainey-Belainey."

I turn my head a little bit toward him. I wish I could be really mean to him so he'd leave me alone, but part of me can't. "Did you have to have a rabies shot?"

"Naw. They asked me a bunch of questions about the squirrel and stuff. No way that squirrel had rabies. Just got a tetanus shot."

"That was lucky."

He nods. "Yup. Hey, my dad says you got calves of your own."

"Yeah."

"Neat! Wish I had some calves."

"You should. Dad got 'em for me to teach me which animal life is worth working to save and which is not. Guess if I need to learn that, you do, too."

He scuffs his feet. "I can help you sometimes."

I feel invaded. The little circle of warmth around

pancakes and Dad and my calves this morning feels threatened already. "That's okay, Jake. Thanks for offering, but Dad wants me to do this all by myself."

"He just means that *he* shouldn't help. He'd probably be glad if it taught me a lesson, too."

"Jake, I'm gonna get to keep the money when we sell these calves. I'm not going to be able to share the money, so it's not fair to share the work. I have to do it. Thanks, anyway."

"It's not for the money. Really, Lainey-Belainey, I don't mind. I'd be glad just to help you. I like calves. And I get home lots earlier than you now with your cross-country. They have to be starving by the time you get home. I can help and we can feed them twice as fast."

The bus is coming, finally.

I turn to face the bus. "That's okay, Jake. Never mind. I'm supposed to do this myself."

The bus brakes are starting to squeal.

"You going to the homecoming dance next Friday night?" Jake asks.

"Hadn't thought about it. No, I guess I'm not," I say. "Are you?"

"Maybe." He scuffs his toe in the gravel. "I'll go if you go," he says.

"Well, I'm not."

"Why not?

"I have to be responsible. Take care of my calves. Won't have time after practice to take care of them and get ready."

"That doesn't take all night, smarty-pants. Especially if you let me help."

I shake my head. "I'm not goin'."

"Lainey," Jake says, "you *sorry* we saved the squirrel?"

I nod my head without looking at him.

"Really?"

I look at him and bite my lip. He knows I'm not sorry. I don't answer, but he can see that I'm not sorry, and he grins.

The bus doors flip open and the bus swallows us down its long aisle. I sit with Melissa Roberts, an eighth-grader who ran sprints on the junior-high track team last year. Jake has to find another seat, farther back in the bus.

Jake doesn't bug me about the calves for the rest of the weekend.

At school on Monday morning, Jailene practically tackles me in the doorway. "Look! Look!" She sticks her hand in my face. There's a Black Hills gold ring on her left ring finger.

"What? Jeez. Settle down."

"It's from Peter, you moron."

"Peter? You guys are *going* together?"

"Yeah. Can you believe it?"

"No, I can't. Kinda fast, huh?"

She shrugs.

I just came in from playing mother to a bunch of calves, like a tomboy, and my best friend has a real boyfriend. I basically told Jake I wasn't even interested in going to the dance, and Jailene is going steady. I feel as if the continental drift is between us, pushing us oceans apart.

I force a smile. "When did you get it?"

"Saturday night."

"Saturday . . . but that was your first date!"

She nods.

"So, what did you do?"

"Saw a movie in Ames. Pizza before, then we had malts at Ruttles afterward."

"How sweet. The classic date."

"Shut up." She whacks me in the arm. "You're jealous."

We grin at each other.

"So, he has his license. How old is he?"

"He just turned sixteen the third of September."

"He's still really old to be a freshman. Is he stupid or something?"

She glares at me. "You really are jealous."

"No, come on. Tell me how he gave you the ring."

"Just pulled it out at Ruttles and said, 'Will you wear this?' and I said, 'You mean go with you?'"

"You idiot."

"Well, I didn't know what to say."

"So you put it on."

"Actually he put it on me."

I raise my eyebrows at her, and she blushes. "Then what?" I ask.

"Then he came around and sat by me in the booth and he kissed me."

"Right there?"

She nods.

"You guys are sick."

"Then we finished our malts, or he finished his—I couldn't swallow much after that—and we sat in the car and he kissed me and . . ."

"And what?"

"And kissed . . ."

"Jail!"

She grins at me.

"Did you tell your mom?"

"What? That he kissed me or that I'm going with him?"

"Either one."

"No! Are you nuts?"

I think of Jake, and for a second, I think it would be better to go to the homecoming dance with him than to be left out of this new world entirely, but I know it would be worse in the long run.

Jailene sighs, holding her hand like she's in a jewelry store commercial. "Do you think you and Amy are going Friday night?"

"Not me."

"You should," Jailene says. "Besides, I'm gonna be a nervous wreck, and I can't only talk to Peter all night. I wish you were gonna be there. You could tell me, too, if we look good together, or stupid or something."

"You and Peter? Why would you look stupid? Isn't it a little late to be worried about that?"

Jailene giggles. "Look. There's Amy. Ame! Come here!"

Amy looks over. Her nose is red. It's cold again this morning, and her fair skin is as sensitive as mercury. "Hi, guys."

"Look." Jailene jams her hand in front of Amy's nose.

Amy squeals. "You lucky, lucky dog." Amy looks at me. "Did she tell you how he kissed her?"

I nod. "As much as I wanted to hear. Come on. I gotta get to my locker."

On the way to homeroom, Amy asks, "So, Lainey, should we go to the dance and watch the lovebirds? Or you think it'll make us depressed?"

"Ha!" I say. "Besides, somebody'll probably ask you."

"I wish Jeremy Sutton would," she says.

"Maybe you should just go," I say. "At least you could stand around and wait for Jeremy to ask you to dance. I don't care if I go or dance or not."

"I'm not going alone!"

"Well, ask Jeremy to go."

"He never talks to me."

"So he's probably shy. Ask him. Or ask somebody, Ame, 'cause I can't go. I've got to take care of my calves."

"That won't take all night. How are the little buggers doing? Spill any more formula?"

I tell her about how the calves don't seem scared anymore when it's time to eat. Amy feels sorry for me having to do all that work twice a day plus cross-country practice.

"I think I like it," I say. I can't quite explain how important those four little babies already are to me.

"I have an idea," Amy says. "What if I ride the after-school activity bus home with you Friday night after you have practice? I can help you feed the calves—that way I get to see them, and then we can get ready for the game and the dance together? Would it be okay with your mom? Think she'd drive us in before the game? My mom could bring you home after the dance."

I'd like to show Amy my calves. Like Jailene showing off her ring, I think. But miles apart. "They're really cute" is all I say. "I'll ask Mom tonight and call you."

Would it be a lie if I told Jake I wasn't going to the dance before I knew I was going? I'm certainly not going to tell him that I'm going. I don't want to go if he goes. What if Amy gets asked to dance a lot, and Jake shows up, too? Every time Amy is dancing, he'll hang around me like he's my boyfriend. I'll die.

In art class, Mr. Reed calls on Jailene twice before she hears him. She's too busy staring at her ring to listen. You'd think Jailene was engaged the way Amy makes such a big deal out of it. There are moments when I'm not sure I even want Amy at my house.

Practice is tough. We run five miles, then coach has us run hill repeats. Five of them, and he's standing in the middle of the hill, making us run faster on each one. My quads feel like Jell-O and I'm gasping, but I make it. I beat everybody on the last two hills. Stacy Ellerbush, the team captain, gives me a look that could kill for beating her, but she's too shot to say anything when I huff past her on the last sprint. "Good job, Lainey," she says when we're done, without looking at me.

I'm soaked with sweat and shivering by the time I get to the showers. Funny how hurting so much can feel so good.

My hair's still wet when I get off the bus. Jake's been waiting for me.

"What do you want?" I ask.

"Can I help you with the calves? You look tired."

I am tired. I'm dead tired. "Jake," I say, "They're not even completely used to me yet. I don't think so." I don't want him invading my warm little circle in the barn. I don't know if I want Amy invading it, either, or how I'll explain it to Jake if he sees Amy come home with me on Friday, but I don't want to think about that yet.

"Come on, Lainey-Belainey, let me help."

My arms ache, my legs ache, and I'd love to just go lie down. But I say, "Jake, I can't." I take off for the house.

I step inside and the door slams behind me.

"Lainey, the door!" Mom yells from somewhere in the back of the house.

"Sorry."

Dad has taken out the screen and put the storm window into the door today. A sure sign of autumn. It smells like molasses in the kitchen. Mom must be in a really good mood, because not only did she give us pancakes for breakfast again this morning but she has made ginger cookies, fresh and warm on the counter, for me after school. I grab four on my way to my room to change. "These are good, Mom. Thanks," I holler.

"It's supposed to frost tonight," she says from the basement stairs. "Dad's coming in to do most of the chores so you and I can save the garden. Please hurry with the calves."

"Okay," I say.

When I go out to chore, carrying my buckets of warm water, Jake is leaning against the houseyard fence as if he's trying to strike a movie star pose. I half expect to see him dangling a cigarette from his lip.

"Hi, sugar pie," he says.

"Don't call me that, Jake." I keep walking toward the barn.

Jake follows me. "Let me carry one of those," he says. I ignore him. When I reach the barn door and he's still with me, I turn to face him. "What do you want, Jake?"

"Free country, ain't it? Can't I walk where my daddy works?"

"Not if your daddy isn't *at* work."

"He's at work all right. He's in the field, Miss High-and-Mighty. You tellin' me to get off your property, ma'am?" He fakes a southern drawl, and he does it badly.

"Shut up, Jake. Of course not. You know I said I have to take care of the calves alone."

"I'm not your daddy. I just wanna see 'em. And I'm not gonna wreck your responsibility by helpin' you."

"I *want* to do this alone."

"Just let me watch, then. Did your daddy say, 'Now be sure you don't let Jake touch these calves or look at 'em'?"

"No, of course not."

"So you aren't disobeying him."

I sigh. "I need some space, okay? Everywhere I go, there you are. I'm getting crap at school for skipping first period with you last week. I'm getting crap at home. Kids at school think we're boyfriend and girlfriend."

"So?" he says.

"Jake! I just want to take care of my calves alone, okay?"

"Sure, fine. I'm just like skunk stink, right—everywhere you go, it sticks to your clothes?"

I can't help grinning. "Something like that, yeah."

He sees me grin and says, "So if I leave you alone, will you go to the dance with me Friday night?"

"Give it up, Jake." I look him square in the eye. "No." I turn away and add, "I'm not going. Now I gotta get to work." I let myself into the barn, close the door behind me, and latch it from the inside. Why didn't I leave it with "no"? I guess that settles that. I am not going to the dance. I'll just have to tell Amy.

The calves are milling around the pen when I come into the barn. They recognize me, and they're not scared of me anymore, although it's easy to spook them. When I mix the powder into the warm water, they can smell it, and they all come over to me right away. They nudge the pail, but they're not too pushy. When they get just a little bigger, it will be a problem. They empty two pails completely. I'll have to start bringing a third one tomorrow.

When I'm done, I hold a little of the calf supplement out to them in my hands. They lip it, and Bambi gets some in his mouth. His head bobs up and down as he chews it and chews it. The rest of us laugh at him. At least I do. Herby stretches his neck to check what is in Bambi's mouth and it looks as if they're kissing. The white-tan calf's name is Thumper because he bumps against the fence with his butt as he backs away from me when he's not eating. He's still the shyest of the four, so I make sure to give him an ear rub before I change the water in their little fountain and leave the barn to take the empty buckets to the house.

CHAPTER 10

As I latch the barn door, I see Mom outside, pulling the little red coaster wagon from the garage. The thing is thirteen years old and rarely gets used, so she wipes it out with a rag, trying to clean it, or at least get rid of the loosest flakes of peeling paint and rust.

I take the milk buckets to the basement and wash them out, then I get a bushel basket from a peg on the wall and join her in the garden.

"It does smell like frost," she says, piling green tomatoes into the wagon.

I wade through the tangled squash vines, retrieving white butternut squash that sit like fat-bellied buddhas, hiding in the vines as if they think they are immune from earthly elements. If we left them here, they would be wrinkled and sagging tomorrow. When my basket is full of squash, I help Mom hunt for tomatoes.

We haul our loads to the basement, where Mom has

spread newspaper all over the pantry shelves that aren't full of her summer canning. We set the tomatoes out carefully on the newspaper. She lays another paper over the top of them when the shelf is full. It's a myth that tomatoes ripen best in the sun when they're off the vine. Most of these will ripen beautifully here, and we'll have fresh tomatoes well into early November if we're lucky.

The squash are set in a big crate in the corner of the room. Then we go back to the garden for more.

When we finish the squash and tomatoes, we dig up the rest of the onions but leave the carrots. They can stand freezing temperatures as long as they're in the ground. Last year, I dug carrots out from under the snow, fresh and juicy, for Thanksgiving dinner. We pick one last overripe bowl of brown string beans. Mom will use the seeds inside the pods for soup.

Finally, we bring our last load to the house. Only then, Mom covers her flowers and her two prize rosebushes with old sheets and blankets. The practical, useful stuff had to be done first. I go to the barn to help Dad finish the chores so he can get back out to the field.

No feeling in the world compares with the night of first frost. It's my favorite night of the year. It smells like harvest, and tomorrow the leaves will start turning.

•   •   •

I'm working on some algebra equations while Mom fixes supper. When she asks me to move my books and set the table, I want to say that I'm too tired to move, but I do what she asks and say, "There's a dance Friday night at school. It's homecoming."

"Oh. Are you going?" She sounds thrilled that I'm considering a social life.

"Not if I'm as tired as I am now."

"Seriously. Do you want to?"

I tell her Amy's scheme, but I explain that I know she's too busy this time of year to be bothered with an unnecessary trip to town, and I expect her to put a kibosh on the whole thing, but her face lights up. My heart sinks. No easy excuse. I tell her about Jailene and Peter, hoping she'll worry that Amy, Jailene, and I are growing up too fast and change her mind. Instead, she asks me if there's a boy I want to dance with. Great.

"Me? No. In fact, I don't want to go at all. I was kind of hoping you'd say no. Jake asked me if I was going, and I said I wasn't."

She stops stirring the gravy on the stove and turns to me. "And just what, young lady, do you expect?"

"What do you mean?"

"You mess around with him, roughhouse with him, you roll around on the ground with him and come back with his blood on your shirt . . . You're too old for him only to think of you as a tomboy!"

"So I can't be friends with somebody without them thinking I'll be their girlfriend?"

"You have to be careful, Lainey."

"Well, I don't want to dance with him. In fact, I don't want to go to the dance at all if he's going to be there."

"You can say no if he asks you."

"Right."

"You just say no to him."

"I already said no, Mom. Jake has a way of wearing you down. The whole dance would be miserable 'cause he'd keep hanging around and he'd keep asking and asking and asking."

Mom eyeballs me. "You should have thought of that before."

"I did. I say no to him almost every blasted day. Besides, *you're* the one who insisted on inviting the pervert over here for every single meal then made me walk him home."

"There's a difference between being neighborly and courting trouble, young lady." She turns back to the counter to dish up the gravy. "So, you can tell Amy I'll take you girls in to the game if you want." I don't remember ever feeling like I hated her this much before.

After supper, I call Amy and tell her Mom said it was okay, even though I'm pretty sure I don't want to.

"Sure you do," Amy says. "We don't want to miss it. Gotta watch Jailene with Peter, you know."

It's dark out, and I'm reading my assignment for American studies. I can barely keep my eyes open. Mom has a batch of green tomato jam on the stove and is getting ready to put two green tomato pies in the oven. They sound horrible, but they taste like apple, and they're actually very good. Dad is out combining corn until late. Here in the house it smells cozy and homey. Raymond, Jake's dad, is driving wagons of corn from the combine and auguring them into the steel bins in the barnyard. We're like squirrels storing acorns on a grand scale.

I can hear Raymond start up the big Allis-Chalmers and head toward the field for another load. The dryers inside the corn bins drone into the night like giant locusts.

And then, through the closed windows and doors, over the whir of the dryers, I can hear banging in the barn and the faint bleating of calves. Mom stops, rolling pin poised in midair, and we look at each other. I jump out of my chair, grab my jacket from the hook by the back door, and fly toward the barn. I'm glad for my long legs, I'm glad for the moon's brightness, I'm glad for the yard light, and I think about each of these things as if I'm watching myself be the hero in a movie going to save somebody. I use the scene in my head to distract myself from being terrified of what is happening to the calves.

I hear a gunshot and I stop. I look toward the field. The combine lights are on, creeping over the ground like a devouring mantis, and Raymond's tractor lights keep moving steadily toward the combine. Dad and Raymond are almost a mile away, so I'm on my own. Behind me, Mom comes out of the back door so fast she lets it bang shut. She catches up to me and walks with me toward the barn.

I can hear wild thumping and banging, then quiet. We keep steadily taking steps toward the barn. I can hear both of our hearts pounding. I should be running, but I'm too scared to move that fast. Some maniac is out here with a gun, and I don't want to go charging into the line of fire. I should have brought a gun, too, but if I took the time now to go back to get one, whoever is out here will be long gone. We keep moving, and I reach the barn door without seeing anyone. It's still latched, so I step around to the side of the barn with Mom beside me, and there's movement in the shadows. In the moonlight I can see the smooth long glint of a gun barrel. I suck in my breath, and the person whirls toward us, gun barrel flashing. We freeze.

"Lainey-Belainey!" A voice comes out of the darkness.

"Jake? Jeez! You scared us to death! You moron!"

"You got coyotes," he says.

"Coyotes? In the barn?"

"No, but tryin' to get in. I saw them nosin' around the door, and one was jumpin' at that low window." Jake points his gun barrel at a window not far from the calf pen.

"Jake," Mom says, "does your father know you have the rifle out tonight?" She looks pale in the moonlight.

"Sorry, Mrs. Ehler."

"Not funny, Jake, you moron," I say.

"Wasn't trying to be. Would you rather the coyotes ate your precious baby calves?"

"They can't get the calves. The windows and doors are closed tight. And the open ones aren't big enough for a coyote."

"Don't be too sure about that."

Jake moves in the general direction of his house, but Mom steps in front of him. "Young man."

He stops, eyes wide at her tone, which I know well but he's never heard before. "You will never, I repeat, *never* fire that gun in this barnyard again, you understand?"

"Yes, ma'am." He slings the gun in the crook of his arm and slinks into the dark.

CHAPTER 11

Dad comes home while I'm still reading in bed. I'm so tired I can hardly move, but I can't let go of the image of Jake and his gun outside the barn. Dad may be angry that I'm still awake, but I drag myself out of bed and go down to the kitchen anyway and plunk onto a kitchen chair to talk to him.

"Lainey! What are doing still up?"

"Do coyotes come up to the barn?"

"Almost never. Worried about your calves?"

"Sort of."

"Did you think you saw one?"

"N-no."

"Don't worry. No self-respecting coyote would come around our buildings with all the ruckus of our tractors going and coming, and the augers and dryers running. Besides, they've got plenty to eat with all the deer and rabbits running from the combines."

Mom walks into the room to hear the last bit of that. We look at each other.

"Why?" Dad asks.

"Jake said he saw one," Mom says.

I get up and move toward the stairs. I stop in the doorway when Dad asks, "Where did he say he saw this coyote?"

"Right by the barn. Raymond had just left the barnyard with an empty wagon."

"I doubt it. Musta been seeing things."

Mom says, "We heard a gunshot, so we went out to check."

"He shot at it? That little . . . He fired a rifle at it?" Dad's face gathers a thundercloud look, and he picks up the October *Wallace's Farmer*, dismissing me. He rolls it up instead of opening it, though, and while I hurry upstairs I hear him tapping it against the edge of the kitchen table. Just as I'm drifting off to sleep, I hear the high-pitched beeps of the phone being dialed.

In the morning, the grass is iced with crisp white frosting, and I break the spines of many tiny grass blades under my feet. I can see my breath on the way to the barn.

•   •   •

I manage to avoid Jake until Friday when Amy comes home with me on the activity bus after practice. As soon as the bus accelerates down the road, Jake steps out of the orchard to meet us.

"What?" I ask.

"I smell a rat," Jake says. "A big rat."

I keep walking. I can feel Amy looking from me to Jake, baffled. Jake steps in front of me, so I have to stop.

"What did you tell your old man, anyway? He told me I'd better stay away from your barn, stay out of the barnyard completely."

"So stay out," I say, trying to step around him.

"You're a snitch," he says. "A big smarty-pants rat."

"You are so warped, Jake." I stare him in the eye. "Do you think I had to say anything? My mom told Dad you shot a rifle at a coyote right next to the barn. Did you really think my mom wouldn't tell him?"

"And what's Miss High-and-Mighty Amy doing here, smarty-pants? Thought you had to take care of your calves all by yourself!"

"Shut up, Jake. This is different." Amy and I start up the driveway.

"You'll get yours, Miss Smarty-Pants. Don't think you won't." We move away from him, the gravel crunching under our feet. "Amy," he calls, "your friend there can't be trusted. Don't tell her any secrets." We walk faster. Finally, from a distance, Jake yells, "Lainey-Belainey, there really was a coyote. Let 'em eat your calves then."

"He gives me the creeps," Amy says when we finally get away from him.

Amy likes the calves, and she has had enough sense to bring old clothes and shoes so she can jump right in and help me. It's fun to show the little guys off and to have help with them. We feed them two at a time.

The football game is fun, loud, and chilly. Perfect football weather. Amy and I keep looking for Peter and Jailene, but we never find them. We want hot dogs, but Amy says our breath will stink for the whole dance if we do that, so we settle for popcorn and hot chocolate. Our school wins the game by four touchdowns and an extra point each time, so it isn't too exciting.

The dance is a pain, at least at first. Everybody lines up by the walls of the gym as if we're picking teams for soccer in PE. I feel like a fly clinging on the wall, waiting to be swatted by seventy pairs of eyes. I can't see Jailene anywhere.

The first song is slow, and only three couples dance. Then Jailene and Peter walk out onto the floor. Jailene is wearing a new, very tight, very red, very miniskirt, and she looks very nervous. Amy jabs me in the ribs as if I haven't noticed her. Over Peter's shoulder, Jailene catches our eyes, and I can't tell if her look is one of ecstasy or panic. Then Peter pulls her near and her eyes close. As I watch her mold her body against his, it hits me that they must have spent a lot of time in each other's arms, because even the embarrassment of dancing in front of the whole school doesn't erase the fact that they are familiar and comfortable being this close. In that instant, I know that they've done more than kiss, that they've been closer than this, maybe lots of times already. They move as if they belong locked together. Jailene used to tell me everything, but I never heard about anything more than her first kiss. Maybe when you get past that first stage, you stop talking about it. She's in a world that I don't know, and all I can do is watch from the sidelines.

The four sets of bodies lock and sway together, and I'm embarrassed that I'm staring. It makes me think of Jake, and I feel my face get hot. I hate him for invading my head at a time like this. I'm glad the lights are low, and I am glad, glad, glad that Jake hasn't shown up. I wonder if some girls date people like Jake because they want to feel that closeness at any cost, and they think it's better to be with a jerk than with no one at all.

The couples are all mashed together as close as they can get, and I think of Jake holding me from behind, trying to touch me. I don't want to think about it, and I don't want to put those two things together in my head, but in spite of myself, I feel the heat rise in my body the way it tingled when Jake held me down and ran his finger along my rib cage. I hate my body for responding when I don't want it to. All this would be so much easier if Jake were all-good or all-bad. Then I could just hate him, or maybe even let myself like him. As it is, he's just good enough to keep me from hating him entirely. I wonder if sometimes girls get touched that way and are so starved to feel good that they give in to guys who are worse than Jake. Why does it have to be so blasted complicated, anyway?

The music saves me by changing. The DJ gears up a fast hip-hop song, and the couples on the dance floor reluctantly pull apart after the slow dance like Silly Putty, clinging to each other by their hands, fingertips, or hips, not wanting to break the strand of physical connection.

None of us can stand still with the beat blaring, and

Meredith Baker and her consort of miniskirt-clad friends swarm onto the floor, gyrating and shaking their shapely little hips and arms and their smooth bouncy breasts. The gym floor fills with bodies following their lead.

"Come on," Amy says, giving me a shove. She pushes me out onto the floor, and she's right behind me. I'm a bad dancer, and I don't know this song very well, but I try to imitate Amy. There are so many bodies all over the floor right now, it doesn't matter that I feel all knees and elbows like a lanky calf.

After two more fast songs, another slow one sends us back to the walls, and there are lots more couples now. They've probably found each other in the sea of the last three songs' gyration. When the beat picks up again, everybody flows back out into the rhythm that fills the gym.

I spot Arcadia Knowles across the floor. She is definitely the coolest person in our whole school. She's dancing all alone, off to the side. I'd never have the guts to dance alone where everyone could see me like that, but she's really good. She dances funky, fast, and strong. She's so good, it makes me think she could get a job in the music video business. She's wearing stretch shorts and a sleeveless, loose, black mini-dress that flares out from her waist when she spins around. It's not like anything anyone else is wearing. She has a red stone nose-ring on tonight that looks like a drop of blood. Her legs look powerful and her muscles are cut, defined on her shoulders, biceps, thighs, and calves without a discernible ounce of fat. Her sleek black hair hangs straight to the bottom of her chin during school, but now, it flares out like her skirt as she spins. I figured by the reddish roots that her hair is dyed, so it's surprising that it shines so much. I try not to stare, but she moves as if she's performing, and other people turn to dance so they can watch her, too. She seems oblivious to her fans, like I thought she was oblivious to the rest of us in class. I'm still amazed that she noticed me in English.

The DJ has noticed her, too, and I get the feeling he was going to play a slow dance but then changed his mind. Almost everyone is dancing now, or at least moving around, but Arcadia is in charge of the dance floor. The DJ slides in a song with a slower pace, and everyone goes nuts screaming and yelling because they know the words. Arcadia slows her movements to fit the music, but every motion is strong and deliberate. I don't think I've seen her do the same move twice.

The whole floor is bedlam for the next two fast songs. I can't see Arcadia, and I forget myself in the movement until I feel a hand on my shoulder. I shudder, thinking it's Jake. I whirl toward the hand, ready to slap him.

It's Arcadia, grinning at me, sweat glistening on her temples. She doesn't even change her rhythm to touch me, but I've stopped moving.

"Hi, Lainey."

"Hi." I feel Amy's eyes on me, accusing me of withholding information. Over the music, I yell, "Arcadia, this is Amy."

"I know."

"Hi," Amy says to Arcadia, but her eyes come back to me, questioning me. I grin and shrug and we three dance in a circle. I feel awkward by comparison. It's impossible not to follow Arcadia's moves, but I'm too aware of her to lose myself in the music and the beat.

"Where'd you learn to dance like that?" Amy asks when the music is a little quieter.

Arcadia shrugs and say, "Jazz lessons, mostly."

"You're really good," I say.

The music slows, and the crowd is pulled into two parts: couples, and all of the rest of us stuck to the wall again. Only three slow-dancing couples show up on the dance floor this time. I see Mrs. Prebyl eagle-eyeing the line around the gym for stray pairs of people who were plastered together earlier; when she doesn't see all of them, she slips out the door. She will go ferret them out of some dark hallway. They think they've slipped away, unnoticed, and are hidden in the shadows by the lockers. Or maybe they've left the dance entirely, gone off in a car to be really alone. I'm glad it's not Jailene. I'd be embarrassed to death for her if it were. But she's safe out on the dance floor, clamped tight against Peter.

When the next fast dance starts, Peter and Jailene pick up their pace, but they stay pasted together. They are like mating dragonflies, stuck together. The scary part is that they'll even fly away intertwined at the end of the night.

After a long set of fast songs and a final slow song, I've lost sight of Arcadia, and I'm relieved when it's eleven o'clock and we can go outside and climb into Amy's mom's white Grand Am.

When her mom asks how the dance was, Amy and I tell her all about Arcadia, but we don't volunteer any information about Jailene. It's an unspoken rule that we don't want her thinking that's how we would act if we had boyfriends. When she asks if Jailene danced with Peter, we just say yes.

When Amy and her mom drop me off, I can smell

fall—the dry leaves and cornstalks toasted from a summer in the sun, the scent of drying grain—and I can see the combine lights halfway across the section where Dad will be out working as late as he can. It's dangerous to operate such huge machinery if you're sleepy. He can't always start in the early morning hours because the cornstalks are often too damp with dew or frost, depending on the temperature. So he waits until the stalks are dry and goes as late as he can into the night.

Amy runs into the house to get her school bag and clothes. I walk her back to the car. "Thanks for the ride and for helping feed the calves," I say into the car before I slam the door. "See you Monday, Amy."

They pull out of the driveway, and I run up the steps and open the back door. I stop on the top step, with the door halfway open. I can hear uneasiness in the barn. Something can't be right when there's this much noise. Peace in the barn is an audible thing, full of contented chewings, nosings, and gruntings. Hunger disrupts the peace in early morning or late afternoon. Any other time, this kind of banging, bleating, and squealing means surprise or fear. I'm frozen for a moment, deciding what to do, then I know I don't have a choice. The babies are my responsibility, and I need to see what's going on. I let the door bang shut and turn toward the barn, walking quietly.

I'm wearing my Levi's (with the tiny hole by the back pocket that Mom sort of mended) and my favorite shirt. It's the dark teal one my aunt Jessie gave me for Christmas, but I have my jean jacket on to protect it and I'll be careful and won't even get in the pen, so I'll stay clean. If there's a coyote, I should have brought a gun, but I can scare it away with enough racket.

The stars are bright, and the combine light is like a giant star that landed on the ground and is slowly creeping the length of the field. Usually it's a comfort to know Dad's out there, but now he seems an eternity away.

I walk without making a sound. I'm good at it because, when I was little, I had a fascination with American Indians. I rode my Shetland pony bareback and practiced walking without a sound, ball of the foot before the heel, like books said the Indians did. The ground is soft tonight, not frozen, so it's easy to be quiet.

In the yellow circle of yard light, a coppery brown tail disappears around the corner of the barn. A coyote. Jake was telling the truth. I'm torn between running to get Dad's .22, to go after the coyote, and running to the barn to make sure the calves are okay. My legs choose for me. I'm running toward the barn.

My shoes crunch the gravel faster and faster. The barn noises have reached a crescendo of fear.

I look on the side of the barn where the coyote disappeared, where Jake was when he shot at one. Nothing. No bright eyes in the dark, and the tail is gone. I can hear the calves' bleats, blending with the other animal noises, and I step back and pull open the barn door. The two single-bulb lamps Dad leaves on all night give the only light in the expanse of barn. I pull the door shut carefully behind me and stand, blinking, letting my eyes adjust before I take a step.

There's someone standing in the calf pen. I suck in my breath. It's Jake. He hasn't seen or heard me over the din of the calves. I stop myself from screaming at him so I can get closer and see what he's doing.

I crouch and sneak down the aisle between pens, but I can't see Jake from this angle. The barn is filled with the rustling of straw, the banging, squealing, baaing, and bleating, and I don't know if the unrest is from the coyote or Jake. A sow lets a feeder lid drop with a sharp metal clang, and the pigs grunt and jump. The sheep are milling around in their social groups instead of lying in huddles, chewing in their half sleep like they normally would at this hour. I sneak closer, trying to see Jake.

He's standing, rocking back and forth, and one hand grips the top rail of the pen. I can hear him groan, and he tips his head back. The calves are standing around him, nudging him, and he still hasn't heard me, so I stand up and move closer, putting my feet ball, heel, ball, heel. When I am twenty feet away, I can hear him breathing hard, then Flower sees me and lets out a happy bleat. Jake jumps. He looks at me with terrified eyes and jerks away.

"What the hell do you think you're doing?" I half scream, half hiss. "Get away from my calves, you perverted son of a bitch!"

Jake looks scared and ashamed while he zips up his pants. I can almost see him push those feelings away until he looks angry and even dangerous. "I thought I heard you go into the house. Little Miss Smarty-Pants trying to trick me? What are you doin' out here, spyin' on me?"

I stare at him, wishing my eyes could become daggers and slice him to ribbons.

"Get out, Jake! You're not supposed to be in here."

He swings one leg over the gate nearest me. I move toward him, and when his feet hit the barn floor outside the pen, I pull my elbow back and let my fist fly up harder than I ever have in my whole life. I feel the bones of my fist against Jake's jaw. My fingers hurt, but I let my fist fly again, straight at his nose. Something bends and snaps, and I'm not sure if it's his nose or my fingers.

Or both. My other fist is already going toward his stomach, and even the pain in my right fist doesn't stop it. My left hand jams into his belly, and he doubles over with an *oof* and slumps to the floor. I have to stop myself from kicking him. I want to turn him into pulp.

Instead, I back up and consider leaving him here and burying him in manure, but I'm afraid of what he would do to the calves when he digs out and gets up. He's curled in a ball, holding his nose with one hand, blood trickling through his fingers, holding his stomach with the other.

"Come on. Get up! You perverted trespassing piece of slime." I poke him in the hamstrings with my foot, really hard. I guess it's a kick, not a poke.

"Just leave me alone. Get the hell away from me. You don't know what it's like," he mumbles.

"What? No idea how it feels to be slime?"

He curls into a tighter ball, and for a moment I feel panic that I have caused serious internal damage. Maybe he'll die. "Get up," I say with a little less fury in my voice.

He rolls to a sit, hugging his knees with one arm and holding his nose with the other. I did this to him, and it's scary how good it feels. He turns his face to look at me through his fingers, his hand still holding his nose.

"You tell," he says in a nasal, gurgly voice, "and I'll kill you."

"Kill me? You're in a fine spot to make threats."

"You don't get it, do you?" He grabs the fence behind him and, leaning on it, drags himself to his feet.

"Move it," I say. "Get out. Go find a doctor."

"You don't get it. I got nothing to lose now, Lainey-Belainey," he says through his hand, still doubled over. "If you tell anybody, I'll kill you. Don't forget. I will, too."

"Tell what, Jake? That you were trespassing? That I beat you up? That I found you with your pants—"

He moves toward me in a rush, blood flying from his nose. He's weakened enough that I can sidestep him and kick at the same time. We both hit the barn floor as he grabs my foot, but I bounce back up and he's down again.

"I'm gonna shoot you," he says from the floor, "with the twenty-two."

I try to laugh. "You can tell everybody you thought I was a coyote."

"You think you're so smart." He glares at me. "You don't know . . ." He pauses to wipe at the blood that's running over his mouth. "You don't know I was in Eldora for manslaughter. So I can do it."

I back up a step. It feels like he punched me in the stomach. And my hand hurts like crazy. "Manslaughter?"

"It might be when you're sleeping," he says. "Or some night when you come out of the barn, or when you've gotten off the school bus." He pulls himself to a stand against the gate. "But I *will* kill you, if you tell. You better watch it. Whenever you're alone. I've done it before. And if you tell anybody why I was in Eldora— especially your mom and dad—you're dead, too."

He wipes his mouth with the back of his hand. "I think you broke my nose. See, I've got nothin' to lose. If you tell your dad what I was . . . that I was in the barn, I'll go back to Eldora anyway 'cause your dad would send me. If I kill you—if they find your body, and they figure out I did it, which is doubtful—they'll send me back there for sure, only I'd be in the security unit and I'd have respect. Murderers get respect. Trespassers and perverts don't. So if you tell, I need to kill you. The only way we both win is if you keep your mouth shut. Got it?"

"You're crazy," I say because I don't know what else to say. I'm hanging on to the pen beside me with my left hand to keep from shaking.

"No. I'm not crazy. I've got nothin' to lose," he says again.

"Except the person who used to be your only friend."

"You lied to me. You're not my friend," he says.

"So you'd kill me?" I wonder if killing him right here, right now, could be considered self-defense.

"You don't deserve to breathe. You said you weren't going to the dance—said you couldn't have help with the calves. That was just to keep me away, wasn't it?" He steps toward me. "But you can go to the dance with Amy, and Amy can help you with your damn calves."

"Jake, I didn't know I was going to the dance when I told you I wasn't. Amy and Jailene talked me into it."

"Of course you don't tell ol' Jake. Don't want him around."

I feel the painful truth of that, and Jake sees it in my face. It's the first advantage he's had, and he shoves my shoulder. "I should've never trusted you."

I stumble, off guard, and catch my balance against the gate with my bad hand. The pain from my fingers shoots up my wrist.

"Lainey-Belainey." He gives me the blackest look I've ever seen. "I will kill you, if you tell." Then he turns and walks out of the barn, holding his nose and leaving the door hanging open behind him.

With my good hand, I rub my calves' faces. They all look okay, so I follow him out and watch him slinking across the barnyard toward his house. "Jake!" I yell after him, holding my throbbing hand, "Prebyl's right. You are irreparable after all." I can't think of anything to say that could hurt him worse. I see his shoulders stiffen, and he walks faster.

I sure hope his nose is broken. I kick at the dirt all the way to the house. I'm not sure why I have tears in my eyes.

"Lainey!" When I'm inside the door, Mom's voice jerks my head up so my eyes meet hers. "Lainey! What happened?"

"I'm tired, Mom. I need to go to bed."

"I heard the door slam, and I started talking to you," she says with a chuckle, "but you weren't there. Did you go check on the calves?"

"Yup. Mom . . . Jake was . . ." Suddenly I'm shaking. I want, need, to tell her. But what if he really is telling the truth? I don't dare . . .

"Jake was what?"

"The dance wasn't worth it. Well, some of it was fun."

"Was Jake there?"

"No. He—he was outside when I got home, and he's furious that I told him I wasn't going."

"You should have told him the truth." She reaches out to touch my hair. "Lainey! How'd you get all full of straw?"

I give my head a shake and step into the kitchen, holding my hand. "I don't know. The barn, I guess."

I try to give her a quick smooch to get past her so she won't see how messed up I really am. "Night, Mom."

"Need anything to eat?" Then she sees me in the kitchen light. "Good Lord! Lainey, what happened out there?"

I want to tell her so bad I almost cry, but I'm too scared, and I have to figure out what to do, so I say, "Nothing. I—I didn't turn the barn lights on and I fell. I'm too tired, I guess." Then I remember. "Mom! I saw a coyote. Right next to the barn."

"No! So he was telling the truth."

I nod. I feel sick.

"Well, go to bed, honey. You look awful."

I go upstairs, close the bathroom door, and look

in the mirror. I can't believe Mom didn't see the blood on my shirt or notice my hand. It's already swollen. One-handed, I peel off my jeans and shirt and flop on my bed. My hand hurts. Bad. The room is spinning.

Somewhere on the outside edges of the spin, I hear a knock downstairs on our door.

"Jake!" I hear my mom's voice. "What happened to you?"

" . . . in a fight," I hear.

"I swear," Mom says, "I've been around boys all my life, but I've never seen anybody get as bloody as often as you." I hear water running in the kitchen. "Your nose just won't stop bleeding," she says. "Jake, I'm pretty sure it's broken. We'll have to get your dad to take you to the emergency room."

"He's out in the field."

"Maybe Lainey can go find him."

My hand is throbbing, and the thought of running over the cornstalk rows in the dark is too much.

"Lainey! Are you in bed yet?"

I get off the bed, but I can't answer. I rush into the bathroom, and, holding my hand, I kneel by the toilet.

"Lainey!" Mom calls again. "Can you go look for Raymond? Jake needs a doctor."

I lean over and lose it all into the toilet. I retch and retch and retch. Then I collapse on the bathroom floor with my bad hand on my chest and a wad of toilet paper in my left fist to dab at my mouth. The room closes down around me into a single pinpoint of light.

"Lainey, are you all right?" I open my eyes to see Mom standing over me.

"I'm sick."

"Good Lord. What next?"

I struggle to sit up, holding my right hand carefully so she won't see I'm not using it, and I realize I'm only in my underwear. "I just need to go to bed."

"Lainey. Were you drinking at the dance?"

"What?" I can hardly believe she's asking me this. "Of course not. I just need to go to bed."

She runs her hand over my forehead. "Will you be okay if I go look for Jake's dad?"

"Sure. Just don't leave Jake here."

"He's not going anywhere but where I put him." She gives me a kiss and heads downstairs. Only a mom could kiss a face that's just thrown up.

"Slimeball doesn't deserve medical treatment," I mutter. "Let him rot. Or die."

"What?" Mom asks, halfway down the stairs.

"Nothing. 'Night, Mom."

"G'night, Lainey-Belainey," Jake yells up the stairs in a nasal tone. "Hope you feel better."

"I hate you, Jake," I whisper toward the light from the stairs. I've never hated anybody like this.

CHAPTER 12

The smell of coffee wakes me in the pale early morning, in that time before sunrise when it feels as if I'm looking at the world through blue tissue paper. My right hand is throbbing. My clock says 5:55, and I wonder why Dad hasn't woken me to feed the calves.

I dangle my legs over the side of the bed and sit up to get busy, but my hand feels as if someone's mashed my knuckles in a vise. I can feel Jake's nose crunch beneath my hand, and all the details of last night in the barn hit me in the stomach. It might come right up and out my mouth again, and I pull my feet back up into bed and sink under the covers, holding my hand.

Most of my right hand is purple and blue this morning, and the three middle fingers are as big as Polish sausages. How am I supposed to not tell what happened when everybody sees my hand? Shit. I can almost hear Jake say, "Shoulda thought o' that before ya punched me, smarty-pants."

I stand up, still holding my hand. "Shit." The word comes out as if saying it will have the same effect as biting on a fork: to keep me from screaming in pain. I wonder if the bones in my hand are broken. I can't hide this.

Very slowly, I put my robe on. I go into the bathroom and fill the sink with cold water, then put my hand in the water. It barely takes the edge off. In fact, any movement feels as if the insides of my hand are shifting around. This is crazy. I can't do all my chores with only one hand. Everything's going black and my knees feel weak. I sit on the toilet, try to put my head between my knees, and keep my hand in the cold water. Sitting like that only makes it hurt worse, so I pull my hand out of the water and lean my head down until I'm not dizzy anymore. God, please, I hope Mom told Dad I was sick, so he did the chores this morning and I have a few more hours to figure out what to do.

I get up and put my hand in the cold water again. When I try to move my fingers, only the pinky twitches and sends up a tiny fleet of bubbles. My stiff hand and the bubbles make me think of a dead body under water, and I imagine Jake tying rocks to me after I'm dead and shoving me into the underground culvert where our 120-

acre field borders the far side of the slough. I wonder how long it would take them to find my body. I remember Jake's words: *If they find your body* . . . He's not entirely stupid, and he knows this whole section of land, every place where he could hide me.

Mom's coming up the stairs. I grab a towel to cover my hand. Thank God I had the sense to shut the bathroom door. She stands outside.

"Elaine."

Elaine. Uh-oh. I must be in more trouble than I thought. "Yeah?" I answer. I'm starting to feel dizzy again.

"Are you okay?"

"Not really."

"Still throwing up?"

"No, but I feel crappy."

"Dad's doing the chores. I told him you were sick."

Sigh of relief. "Thanks, Mom."

"Jake's nose is broken."

"Yes!" I whisper toward the ceiling.

The bathroom door opens without me inviting Mom in. "What did you say?" Mom asks.

"Nothing," I say as I pull the drain from the cold water with my left hand, making sure the towel covers my right hand, then pretend to dry my hands slowly. My eyes are watering, it hurts so bad to touch my right hand.

She stares me down until I lift my eyes to meet hers.

"You're glad he broke his nose."

"He deserved it." I want desperately to lift my wounded fist in triumph but everything is going black again. I see her face on a diminishing TV screen. Everything's black around her and is closing in until her face is a tiny dot.

"Jake told me what happened," I hear her say.

"Lainey! Lainey!"

I look up into Mom's face, and far above her is the bathroom ceiling.

"Did I faint?" I whisper.

"What happened to your hand?"

"Can't tell you."

"Yes, you will, young lady."

I shake my head and struggle to sit up. I manage to lean against the edge of the tub, holding my hand.

"You punched Jake." She sighs the way she does after every time I fight with Jake. "Can you move your fingers?"

"Yeah. Look." I hold up my sausages and valiantly wiggle my thumb and pinkie. We look at each other and I almost giggle.

She lets out a sound that could start as a laugh, but she decides not to let me get that advantage. "I'll go tell Dad while you get dressed. If you'd have told me last night, I wouldn't have had to go to the emergency room *twice*."

"You had to take Jake?"

"Raymond was on a late run to the elevator in Cambridge when I got out there."

I get up from the floor, holding on to the side of the tub. "I'm sorry about that. But I wouldn't have ridden in the car with him if it meant feeling like this for weeks. And I think you'd have been just as mad if I'd have told you last night. Plus, I didn't know it was so bad . . ."

She looks at me without saying anything then goes downstairs and outside.

I sit on my bed and peel off my robe. I slept in yesterday's underwear, so I peel that off, too. It's not easy, but it's easier than it is to pull up my jeans and zip them with one hand. I have to leave my bra hanging unhooked. I try to put on a baggy sweatshirt, but my fingers hurt when I try to squeeze them through the cuff of the sleeve, so I pull on a baggy T-shirt.

I run a brush through my hair. I start to black out again while I brush my teeth left-handed. So I sit with my head down, feeling toothpaste run up into my nasal cavity until the blackness goes away. Then I spit and spit and spit and blow my nose one-handed. Mom hooks my bra for me, drapes a jacket around my shoulders, and herds me to the car.

I look at Mom as we pull out onto the blacktop. "So what did Jake say happened?"

"He said he got into a fight after the dance."

"That's it?"

"He wanted to dance with some girl who wouldn't dance with him and he got ambushed after the dance because of it."

"That slime . . ."

"That what?"

"Nothing." Son of a bitch, I think.

I can feel anger filling the car. Mine and hers.

"He didn't say," Mom says, turning onto the main highway into town, "that it was you. Now, are you gonna tell me what happened?"

I shake my head and lean back in the seat. It's a long, long ride into town, and it's a relief to pull up to the emergency room door.

"You're grounded until you tell us why you broke your neighbor's nose."

"'Cause he's a perverted scumbag. I wouldn't dance with him if he were the last guy on earth."

Mom gets out of the car, slams her door, and doesn't look at me as we walk into the hospital. Mom sits at the reception desk to answer questions for the lady by the computer, and they make me sit in a wheelchair and a nurse who doesn't smile whisks me off to the X-ray room.

I have four X rays taken, and I'm getting a splint on two and a half fingers and my whole hand. I broke three little bones, one metacarpal and two phalanges, Dr. Kruse says. He can't put the real cast on until the swelling goes down a little. That means I have to come back tomorrow or Monday. Mom will be thrilled. Already I think she might die of embarrassment about this.

Dr. Kruse asks me if I want a neon pink or green cast when we do the real thing, but I say I'd rather it be white and less conspicuous if he doesn't mind.

"The real cast will look more like a boxer's glove," Dr. Kruse says as he wraps it. He teases me about having a boxer's fracture. "You must pack a powerful wallop." I almost grin. He chuckles and says I'd better quit punching out the boys. I look at him so fast he notices and stops midwrap.

"I was kidding. Who did you punch?" he asked.

I look down.

"Oh," he says, the light obviously coming on. "It didn't happen to be that boy in here with the broken nose last night, was it?" He smacks himself in the forehead with his free hand. "Was it your mom that brought him in? I'm pretty dim not to have put this together before."

I remain silent.

"I'd say the fractures would have taken the same amount of force." He shakes his head. "I've never known a girl who could pack such a punch." He looks at my upper arm, and I curse the fact that I couldn't get a long-sleeved shirt on. "You're really strong for someone so . . . lean. Are you an athlete?"

"I guess, yeah."

"I hope not volleyball. You'll miss the whole season."

"Cross-country and track."

"Yeah, you look like a runner. Well, sorry, but you'll miss most of the cross-country season. You might be able to run with your cast by the section meet. But not at all for at least four weeks so these bones can set. No jostling."

I nod, thinking of my good practice times. I feel myself sinking into the table. Our first big meet is Tuesday in Ankeny. I'll miss it. With that much time off, I'll be worthless at the end of the season.

The doctor sees my face. "Sorry about that."

I shrug. "Thanks." I don't trust myself to say much more than that.

"What on earth did that Riley boy do to you to make you hit him like this? You don't seem like the ornery type, so he must have done something pretty awful."

"He did." I bite my lip and look away. Man, I have to watch my mouth. This could get me in lots of trouble.

He stops wrapping again and supports my broken hand until I look back at him. "I have to write a report of this incident. What's his name—the Riley boy?"

"Jake."

"Yes. Jake Riley told me that he got in a fight after the school dance last night. My guess is he didn't want anybody to know a girl got the best of him."

"He didn't go to the dance," I say, looking down again. "But it was after the dance."

"I think you ought to tell somebody what happened here. Save yourself a lot of grief. What did he do to you?"

"He—he didn't actually do anything to me."

"Did he make sexual advances?"

I shake my head no again, frowning. "Not last night." I wonder how much Dr. Kruse can guess. He's seen a lot of life.

"He has before?"

I nod, scared. "I ran. I hit him then, too."

Dr. Kruse masks a chuckle. "I'll bet he wishes he had learned his lesson back then, huh?""

I nod.

"Can you tell me what happened?"

I shrug and shake my head. I sit staring at the diagram of the human skeleton on the wall.

He starts wrapping again. "Listen, I'm required by law to report injuries to minors. I have to give my interpretation of the wounds, and I have to report that you punched Mr. Riley in the nose, Elaine. I can simply state that you struggled after the dance, and that you punched him in the altercation. My guess is that he provoked you, but since you don't show signs of being wounded by young Mr. Riley, and if he presses charges, he could have a case for assault."

"Assault?"

"Well, did you attack him for no reason or was it self-defense? Defending someone else? What should I say? Previous incidents of sexual assault by Mr. Riley?"

"No! I mean, don't say that. It—it was almost self-defense. It was sort of self-defense."

"Are you going to tell me?"

"I can't."

I watch him frown as he wraps. "It would certainly make things look better for you if you told me why you punched him, but nobody's pressing charges at this point, so I'll just write it as I see it."

Mom does not speak to me the whole way home. She's angry and embarrassed beyond words. The only thing that makes me feel any better is that a broken nose has to hurt worse than broken fingers.

CHAPTER 13

We drive up to the garage as Jake eases himself around the corner. I wonder how long he's been waiting for us. His nose is taped, and I see purple spreading across his face. I think he's going to have two black eyes.

I fling my car door open with my left hand. "What the hell are you doing here?" I slam the door shut with my good hand and go to the garage door to open it. Good thing so many things can be done with one hand.

Jake says, "Did you tell? Am I gonna need to knock ya off, Miss Smarty-Pants?"

"What d'ya think, Jake? All the shit you've pulled . . . have I ever told?"

He says nothing but scuffs the ground with his toe. Mom guides the car into the garage.

"Jake, even the doctor could tell it was me that hit you. He said the force of these breaks"—I hold up my hand—"match the force it took to break your nose. He said I pack a powerful punch." Jake's face turns red behind the purple. "Mom knew in a second."

"You little shit! You told." His hands are in fists, and I wonder what he'd do if Mom weren't in the car.

"No, I didn't. They—both the doctor and Mom—figured it out, tried hard to get out of me why I hit you like that, but I wouldn't tell them."

Jake almost grins.

Mom opens the car door and steps out of the car. She glares in Jake's direction, and he stomps around the corner of the garage, out of her line of sight. He jerks his head, motioning me to follow.

I look at Mom. "Forget it, you pervert," I say.

"Elaine!" she says. "Get in the house right now." Her voice is sharp as she yanks the garage door shut.

At the back door, I turn and see Jake hurrying toward his house like some phantom or troll that can't be seen in the daylight.

Inside the house, Mom's hand flies out and slaps me squarely on the cheek. "You stay away from Jake, you hear? Haven't you gotten yourself in enough trouble with that boy?" Tears bounce to the surface of my eyes from the sting and the surprise of it. My good hand is against my face, holding the shocked skin of my cheek.

"You're the one who made me walk him home,

invited him for dinner! And what would you rather I'd do, Mom? Punch him in the nose or let him have sex with me? Would you rather I'd say yes to everything he wants or punch him in the nose when he doesn't get it?"

I turn and pound up the steps.

"Lainey!" she calls after me, but I slam my bedroom door shut. She hasn't hit me since I was nine.

I take two of the painkillers Dr. Kruse gave me and curl up, with my hand on a pillow, to fall asleep on top of my covers. It takes a little while for the pills to work, and until they do, I wonder what Mom will say to Dad.

Mom shakes me awake at noon. "Dad came in from the field to eat."

"Mom, I'm not hungry. Can I just sleep, please?"

"He parked the combine in the middle of a sunny harvest day just to talk to you. I think you'd better be there."

I splash some cold water on my face and run a brush through my hair.

"Hi, Dad." I plop down on a kitchen chair. Mom has pork chops, baked potatoes, string beans, and green-tomato pie on the table. Dad likes having his biggest meal at noon, "dinner" in the farm tradition, and Mom has gone all out since Dad came in to eat with us while combining is in full swing. I could do without this occasion.

Dad loves pork chops, but he doesn't reach for his food. He picks up his fork and sets it down again. "Lainey. Why did you slug Jake?" There's a glimmer of humor in his eye.

"I got him good, didn't I?"

"Why?" The humor's gone, and that thundercloud look grows in his eyebrows. "Tell me."

"He said he'd kill me if I told."

"That's an empty threat, you know. He wants to scare you. If you don't tell *me*, you *should* be plenty scared."

I feel tears in my eyes, and I hate myself for letting them be there. "I don't really know what he was doing, but . . . but . . ."

"Tell me," Dad says.

"There was a lot of ruckus in the barn when I got home. So I went to check on the calves. Jake was in the pen with the calves. I don't know what he was doing, but when he saw me, he zipped up his pants quick." I can't look at Dad's face. "He said if I told, he'd kill me."

Dad snorts and I look at him. His face is red, he's so angry. Then he starts to shake, and he's chuckling.

"Who-ee. At least I know my little girl can take care

of herself!" He laughs and laughs. "You broke his nose. Can't believe it. Maybe that'll teach him I meant it about staying out of the barn."

"Dad, I'm scared."

"Sounds like Jake is the one who should be scared."

"He figures you'll see to it he gets sent back to Eldora, one way or another. For trespassing, even."

Dad nods.

"So it's better to go in for a murder rap than something else—more respect."

Dad stops short, laughter gone, eyeing me. "Stay away from him, Lainey."

"Don't you think I've been trying? Mom made me walk him home when you were in Chicago. I don't want anything to do with him. Can you send him back to Eldora, please?"

"Lainey," Mom says, "did he really want, I mean, did he really try to . . . or suggest to you . . ." Her face is red and she can't finish her sentence.

"You mean to have sex with me, Mom?"

Mom's hand flies to her mouth, and she nods toward the floor. Dad's face jerks toward mine, at full attention.

"Yes! Why do you think I called him a pervert? I hate him. He grabs at me whenever he can. I'm not *roughhousing*, Mom—I'm protecting myself."

Dad stops all movement. "I'll talk to Raymond."

"Dad, please send him back. If you just talk to his dad, it'll be worse, don't you see? Either call the cops and send him back, or don't say anything, please."

"I think we can take care of this, Lainey. He hasn't done anything that warrants calling the sheriff. If Raymond knows his choices are to make Jake toe the line or move out, something will happen. You watch."

"Dad. Please. You don't understand. He will *kill* me. He doesn't lie." I stare at him in horror. Dad doesn't seem impressed. "Please, Dad, don't say anything to Raymond yet. Please."

"I'll take care of it, Lainey. Just stay away from him, and it'll be okay." Dad picks up his fork and knife and attacks a pork chop.

I have no appetite. "Mom, I'm not hungry. May I be excused?"

She nods, and I take the stairs slowly. With every step, my legs feel like lead and my broken bones shoot pain up my arm.

On Monday morning at 8:05, I'm in the outpatient waiting room, missing first period at school so I can get my full cast.

I pick up a copy of *Runner's World*, and there's a

short article inside about a high-school junior who ran a 5K (3.1 miles) in sixteen minutes and sixteen seconds. I do a little left-handed multiplication. That's an average of about five minutes and sixteen seconds per mile for more than three miles. That's fast.

I wonder if I can run close to a five-minute mile this year. I think I can. Last spring in track, my best time for the mile was 5:40, but my coach already clocked me this year at 5:21 for a practice run. The girl's school record for the one-mile (actually 1,600 meters) is 5:08. I want to beat that—if not this year, next year.

I wonder if I'll be able to run in four weeks with my broken hand, and if it will hurt a lot.

I wonder if Jake would watch me start running and cut across the section so he could kill me a mile from home. Nobody would hear the gunshot then.

I almost don't hear the nurse. "Elaine?"

I answer all her questions. Yes, I had ice on my hand almost all weekend; yes, the pain has subsided a tiny bit; and yes, I've been taking my painkillers every four hours and Ibuprofen in between for the swelling.

She assures me the swelling has gone down enough to put the cast on. She wheels over a portable six-foot-high case of various wrapping strips and plaster. No, I don't want a neon cast in pink or green. I want white.

The doctor breezes in and starts working. I zone out.

"Elaine?" he asks. "Feel any more like talking today?"

"No." I try to smile at him, though. He's being nice to me.

When he's done, he says he needs to see me in about ten days for an X ray and I cannot run for three weeks, probably four, until the bones set.

When we leave the hospital, Mom drops me off at school. She's giving me the silent treatment, because she's still annoyed at me. I think I'm an embarrassment. How many moms want to tell their friends that their daughters got broken bones from punching a boy?

I can't get my white boxing glove through my jacket sleeve, so I have to hang my jean jacket over my shoulders like a cape. I slip the jacket off and carry it over my cast on the way to the office to get a pass and to my locker. After I ditch my jacket, it's impossible to walk down the hall so the cast doesn't show. It's as big around as my thigh.

I didn't do all of my homework because you can't read what I write with my left hand. I did my math very slowly and read my American studies, but even I couldn't read what I'd written for the questions at the end of the chapter, so I gave up after three of them. Besides, the painkillers made me so sleepy I could hardly stay awake.

When I slip into my seat in art class, Jailene asks, "Spend the morning with Jake again?"

I shake my head, trying to give her a look that would kill while keeping my cast hidden between my knees.

We're doing pencil sketches of a bowl of fruit. This is going to be pretty bad since I can't even draw with my right hand. I look at the fruit as carefully as I can. The apple is not perfectly round and has a circle of shine on the front, and the orange's shadow follows the same circle in reverse. I put my left hand on the paper and try to draw two roundish shapes so I can shade what I see. I can hardly make the pencil line connect at both ends of the circle.

"Where were you?" Jailene asks.

"At the hospital." I pull my cast up to rest on my thigh.

She stares. "For crying out loud! What happened?"

"Can't tell you." I try to shade some apple.

I've been practicing this moment for two days, trying to figure out what to say when everybody asks what happened. I haven't been able to come up with a single half-truth that sounds plausible.

I have to be careful what I tell people, in case the truth finally comes out, so people won't think I'm a liar. I don't want to be known as somebody who invents stories. Nobody trusts a liar.

"What do you mean, you can't tell me?" Jailene says.

"I just can't."

She starts to say something else, but Mr. Reed is passing behind us on his stroll around the room. We bend our heads over our drawings.

"Elaine, are you left-handed?"

I swallow. "No."

"Why are you drawing that way, then? This looks like a second-grader's work." The whole class titters. I feel my face flood with red.

I set my cast up on the art table, and the titters change to quiet respect. Everybody pays attention to an honest injury.

"What happened?" Mr. Reed asks on behalf of the roomful of listening ears.

"I broke a few bones in my hand."

"How did you do that?"

"I smashed it in the barn. Broke three bones." At least that's not untrue.

"Well, I don't know how you're going to be able to

manage this class without your dominant hand."

Later, when everyone else has lost interest in my hand, Mr. Reed comes back and says that we'll have to see how much I can do when it comes to clay work and the other projects that will be required before my cast comes off. Good thing we're done with papier-mâché. For now, we both know but don't say that my drawing doesn't look much worse than it would with my right hand.

"What did you really do?" Jailene asks when he walks away. She can't stand this. "Did you really smash it in the barn?"

"I smashed it in the barn."

"So what's the big deal? What aren't you telling me?"

I don't look at her.

She's not talking about Peter. She's asked me seven questions and hasn't said anything about Peter. Maybe she is the same person I've always known. Maybe I can trust her. I sure need to tell somebody who will take me seriously.

I look at her carefully, chewing my lip. Her eyes urge me to tell her. "Shhh. Listen," I say, "swear on your own grave you won't tell?"

"What about Amy? Can I tell her?"

"Nobody. Or I don't tell you."

She shrugs. "Okay."

"He said he'd kill me if I told."

"Who?"

"Jake."

"That's just an expression. Everybody says that—'I'll kill you if . . . '—you know. Forget it. He can't hurt you. Come on, tell me."

I whirl on her in my chair and hiss in a whisper, "With Jake, it isn't just an expression. He means it. I've seen what he can do. He'd shoot me in the night through my window. You've gotta believe me that it's life and death, or I can't tell you."

Jailene's face goes white and she's stopped pretending to draw.

"If I tell you and you know," I say, "I suppose he might try to kill you, too. I hadn't thought of that."

"I won't tell. So he'll never know that I know. Is he nuts or what?"

"Sort of. I punched him in the nose."

"Jake? You punched him?" She starts laughing. "That's it? He'll kill you, if you tell that you punched him?"

"You haven't seen him this morning, have you?"

She shakes her head, shaking with giggles.

"I broke his nose."

"Why? What did he do?"

"You're not gonna believe it. Plus, he told me why he was in reform school."

"Why?"

I lean over so my mouth is so close to her ear that her hair tickles my lips. "Murder."

I grab her leg because I'm afraid she'll fall off her stool.

"Who did he kill?"

"I don't have a clue."

"Do your parents know that?"

I shake my head. "I'm sure he doesn't want everybody knowing a girl broke his nose, but that's just the tiniest bit of it. He said if I told them why he was in Eldora, he'd kill me, and if I told what he did Friday night."

"So what did he do?"

"I'll have to tell you somewhere else. You might puke or something. I can't say it here."

She stares at me.

"Even the doctor figured out that I punched Jake. He wanted to know what Jake did to make me punch him so hard."

"Did you tell the doctor?"

I shake my head again. She considers my face and can see that I mean everything I've said, and she's quiet while Mr. Reed moves past the next table to another corner of the room.

"He must have done something awful."

I nod.

"Are you scared?"

"Yes. Wouldn't you be?"

"Lainey, did he rape you? Or try to?"

"No. Not this time."

"Not this time? Lainey! Are you serious?"

I stare at the empty, lopsided circles on my paper.

"Can you go to the cops?" Jailene asks. "They'd protect you, wouldn't they?"

"I don't think he's committed a crime."

Mr. Reed passes behind us again, so we draw some more.

When he's gone, I say, "Did you have fun at the dance?"

She looks at me without a smile and nods.

"Stupid question," I say. "It was obvious that you were having fun."

She turns bright red.

"Ooh. What?" I ask.

"Nothing." She's drawing furiously. Her apple is

starting to look like a cannonball.

"Listen. Either we trust each other or we don't. What are you not telling me?"

Her apple cannonball has a stem and no light reflection at all. She's going over and over it, shading it so hard that it's getting shiny. Without her lifting her face, I see a tear coming out of the corner of her eye.

"What? Jail, did you guys break up or something?"

She shakes her head and swipes at her eye. "I wish I'd broken up with him. I had my chance."

"Jeez, Jail, you guys looked as chummy as you could get in an upright position on Friday night. What happened?"

"Too chummy. We got too chummy in a horizontal position, if you must know."

"Oh, my God. Did you do it?"

She keeps blackening her circle.

"You did it, didn't you?" My whisper is full of awe.

The tears are coming now.

"Why are you crying? Jeez. I'm sorry," I say. It's too much all at once. I can't even imagine being naked with a boy, when I think of how I felt with Jake just looking at my breasts. And Jailene and Peter have only been going together for a week. I try to imagine her naked with Peter on top of her. I can't.

"Jeez," I say again. I don't get it. On Friday night, she looked for all the world as if she wanted it as bad as Peter did. But now she's crying.

"You tell and I'll kill you," she whispers.

"Very funny. Don't worry. I won't tell."

"Sorry. I won't really kill you." She almost grins, then she pauses. "Well, maybe."

I grin as much as I can manage, which is almost not at all. "I know. And I won't tell."

Jailene and I don't get another chance to talk, and I can't concentrate in any of my classes. Everybody asks me what happened to my hand, and I say I smashed it in the barn and broke a few bones. By fourth period, my hand really hurts again and my whole arm aches from trying to keep my hand elevated when I'm not trying to hide it.

Only Amy bugs me for details about how it happened, as if she thinks she must have narrowly escaped breaking her own hand when she helped me feed the calves. Then, we see Jake's face in the lunchroom.

His eyes are black and a little puffy. I wonder why his dad made him come to school today. He looks like an angry raccoon.

Jailene smacks me in the right arm when she sees

him. "Geez, Lainey." The blow sends a shock of pain all the way from my fingers up to my shoulder socket.

"Ouch!"

"What happened to Jake?" Amy asks.

"He had an accident in the barn," I say before I can stop myself.

She stares at me, eyes and mouth wide open. "It's Jake you smashed your hand against? Seriously?"

"Shut up!" I say, but not fast enough. Three or four people on either side of us in the lunch line hear her and stare at me.

"Lainey!" Amy starts giggling.

Jake looks up and sees us and the whole lunch line looking at him. He knows they know something, and his eyes grab mine as if his gaze is an iron grip.

I turn and run out of the lunchroom.

CHAPTER 14

Amy and Jailene follow me out of the lunchroom and into the girls' bathroom, but, as always during lunch, it's packed with girls crowding around the mirror, so we head down the long hall toward the girls' locker room. We aren't supposed to be down here, but it's the only place we have a chance of being alone. I open the door and there's a whole gym class inside in various stages of shorts, sports bras, and athletic shoes. I let the door fall shut on the smells of deodorant and hair spray.

We end up outside the building. It's too cold to be out here without coats, and the only other people out are the smokers who sneak out and don't bother to go across the street from school property before they light up. We huddle in the corner, trying to keep warm. The sky is gray and cold-looking, as if it could fall down on top of us. I wish it would.

"I'm really hungry," Amy says. "I suppose this means I won't get to eat lunch."

"Tough it out," Jailene says.

Amy shuts up. I look at Jailene. I can tell she doesn't want to talk in front of Amy any more than I do, because we're both worried about Amy's ability to keep her mouth shut. Amy suddenly seems much younger than either Jailene or me.

"So why are we out here freezing our butts off?" Amy looks at us. We both study our toes. "You punched Jake, didn't you, Lainey?" she asks.

"Yeah."

"Is his nose broken?"

"Yeah."

"Why? I mean, what did he do?"

"Amy," Jailene says, "Lainey says that if she tells, Jake will kill her."

"He won't really. Everybody says that . . ."

Jailene punches Amy in the shoulder.

"Ow! Stop it."

"We don't have time here to be stupid. Lainey wouldn't be worried if she didn't think he'd really do it."

"You serious?" Amy faces me. "He wouldn't really *kill* you—"

"Ame!" Jailene says through clenched teeth.

"Gambling about if he *really* means it or not is a little risky, don't you think? If we're wrong, it's way too late—"

I cut her off. "He said something about '*if* they find my body,' and I've seen him use a gun and seen him cut off a squirrel's leg. I know he could do it. And I believe he would—like he says, he's got nothing to lose."

"There's everything to lose. He'd go to jail, or prison. What a moron."

"He's a minor, stupid. He can't go to jail," Jailene says. "He'd go back to Eldora, and he knows what that's like. And first they'd have to prove he did it."

"We'd tell."

Jailene and I look hard at Amy.

"I mean," she shrinks a little, "if you ended up dead, we'd tell."

"Thanks a lot," I say, staring out across the street.

"If he doesn't kill us, too," Jailene says.

"Nobody dies, if I don't tell," I say.

Amy stares at me. "I don't like this."

"You still want to know?" I ask.

"Yes," Jailene says.

Amy doesn't say anything.

"Why don't you go eat lunch," Jailene says.

"Alone? No." Amy sighs. "I'll stay, but I'm awful hungry."

"Go eat, then," Jailene says.

"I wanna know," Amy says.

"You can't . . ."

"I won't tell anybody."

"Amy," Jailene says, "it's more than just not telling. It's pretending that you don't know anything."

Amy nods. "Sure."

"Okay, Lainey, hurry up," Jailene says.

"Okay," I say, "I can't explain all of it now, but . . . God, you can *not* tell *anyone* this! You know he was in reform school before he came here. All we knew was that he was in for fighting. Well, that's not true. He was in for *murder*. See why I know he could kill me?"

Jailene just stares at the ground, and Amy gasps so hard I think her sudden intake of air will knock her backward.

"If I tell stuff about what he's done, he could go back in, but he says the only way to have any respect in there is to go in for murder, so he has nothing to lose. He says he might as well go back in for murder and shut me up forever. And get even with me for putting him back there. It would be like his life is over on a second murder rap. If he doesn't kill me, he'd end up the same place, but without respect, so he's got nothing to lose."

"Lainey," Jailene says, "what did he do?"

"I'm not actually sure."

"What do you mean? Why's he all uptight then?"

"I went into the barn after the dance, and he didn't see me at first. He was in with my calves. When he saw me, he zipped up his pants real quick."

"Oh, yuck. What do you think he was doing?"

"Your guess is as good as mine. I can't really stand to think about it," I say. "But I called him a piece of slime and punched him in the nose, then he said if I told, he'd kill me."

"So it must have been bad."

"First I thought he meant if I told that I broke his nose . . . then there are all those other times that he tried to grab me and I got away."

"He *grabbed* you?" Jailene asks. "What did you do?"

"Hit him or ran. Or both."

Jailene and Amy both look at me with sympathy.

"And then he shot a rifle right outside our barn, said he saw a coyote. We didn't believe him, and Dad banned him from our barnyard, so him being in the barn was trespassing anyway."

"Well, is that enough stuff to send him back to Eldora? I mean, that's not breaking a law, is it?"

The school door swings open and we all jump.

Arcadia Knowles steps out into the crisp air wearing a black turtleneck and black stretch pants and black boots. Her hair is jet-black today, too, all the way to the roots. She must have dyed it since the dance. Her stomach is flat and the only bulges showing through the stretchy material all over her body are muscles in her arms and thighs, and her impressive boobs. Her boobs are like determined tugboats leading a ship. As they float her past us, her eyes meet mine and she grins. "Oh, hi, Lainey. Hi, Amy."

"Hi, Arcadia. Hey, Arcadia, this is Jailene."

"Hi." She looks suddenly bashful, which seems impossible with that body, those dancing moves, and those clothes, but she seems at a loss for words. "Kinda cold out here, huh?"

"Yeah." We sound like a bunch of idiots.

She smiles again and moves past us, down the sidewalk alone. We watch her cross the street and sit on the curb where the smokers go because it's illegal to smoke on school property. I find myself amazed that such an athletic-bodied person would smoke. She reaches into her rattan bag, but instead of cigarettes, she pulls out a thermos and starts drinking.

"Holy buckets," Jailene says. "Think she's got a drinking problem?"

"Why else would she go over there to drink?" Amy asks.

I don't get it. Being an alcoholic seems more impossible for Arcadia than being a smoker, but what do I know.

She sees us staring at her, and we look away quickly.

"Shall we go sit by her?" I ask.

"Are you nuts?" Amy says. "Everybody will think we're druggies, too. Or winos. Besides, I'm starving."

"Go cat," I say. "Just remember: If I drop off the face of the earth, you know Jake did it, so tell the cops, and don't go anywhere alone until they put him away. Okay?"

"Holy buckets," Jailene says again.

"Would you stop saying that?" Amy says. "That is the dumbest—"

"Shut up, Ame," Jailene says. "So, Lainey, what are you going to do?"

"I don't have a clue." We're silent together, and it feels good to have them there, even if I probably shouldn't have told Amy. "So, Jail, what's with you?"

"You don't want to know." Her eyes beseech me not to make her tell in front of Amy, and the door swings open again.

We don't jump like we did before, but when Jake

steps out into the gray sunlight, we freeze. I feel my face turn red, and as he glares at me through his raccoon eyes, I feel the color drain away as if he pulled a plug somewhere in my gut.

"Hi, Jake," I say as calmly as I can. "We were just going in." I start for the door.

"Not so fast," he says, stepping in my way.

"What do *you* want?" Amy asks, and the snottiness in her voice gives me away. Jake's eyes react, and I see that he knows I've told.

"So," he says, "what's so all-fired important that you girls have to have a powwow out here with the smokers?"

"None of your business, Jake," Jailene says. "Come on, you guys." She grabs our elbows in the old chicken-wing hold and steers us around Jake toward the door.

He snaps out his arm and rests his palm again the brick wall, stopping us short.

"Well, then, let me guess. First, Miss Smarty-Pants here is probably bein' stupid and tellin' stories about me that are none of your business."

"Why, Jake?" Amy asks. "Are you paranoid? Is there something you don't want her to tell?"

Jake's eyes narrow. "Lainey-Belainey, I thought you were smarter than that."

"You're sick, Jake. Leave her alone!"

I jab Amy in the ribs, hard.

Jake pretends not to notice. "Second, I figure Jailene here is givin' her version of her love affair with Mr. Studmuffin Peter Stortman."

Jailene and I look at each other. "What?" I say.

"I came out here because I thought Miss Smarty-Pants's friends might find it their business that Mr. Studmuffin Stortman is braggin' like hell in the locker room that he got laid Friday night. Says Miss None-of-Your-Business Jailene is a quite a piece."

Amy reacts first. "What are you talking about? You're lying! And you're such a sicko!" She rushes at him, fists flying.

Jake grabs both her wrists easily, and I realize what a wimp she is.

"Let go of me, you lowdown creep . . . you lying slimebag!" she screams.

He shoves her back to us again, and we hang on to her.

"You think I'm lyin'?" Jake asks Jailene.

Jailene's face is white and stony as porcelain. She says nothing.

"Come on. We don't have to listen to this." I let go of Amy with my left hand and grab Jailene. I shove Amy toward the door with my cast. "Jake, this is mean. You have no idea. We're going in."

"Didn't mean to be mean, Lainey-Belainey. I thought I was doin' your friend a favor. Thought Jailene might want to know what her boyfriend's really like. I'd want to know if somebody stabbed me in the back. Tellin' stories without me knowin'. That's all I came out here for."

We step around him toward the building, and he lets us go.

"Lainey?" Jake says quietly, and I turn my head toward him, not looking at him but listening with my head turned even as Jailene pulls me another step toward the door. "Didn't expect to find you tellin'. Thought you really wouldn't."

Amy flashes her middle finger at him, and Jailene shoves her to the door just as it swings open from the inside. It misses Amy's forehead by less than an inch.

Mrs. Prebyl steps out.

"Oh, shit." It comes out of my mouth before I can stop it. She catches Amy with her finger aimed at Jake, but we are lucky that's all she saw. Even so, she won't let us, particularly me, off easy.

"Excuse us," I try to say brightly.

Her made-up face doesn't crack a smile. She's in a

sailor-suit dress today, with big navy blue anchor earrings. I'd like to grab one and yank on it, but I restrain myself.

"Hold it, girls," she says, eyeing my cast. "What's going on here?"

"Nothing, absolutely nothing. We just had a little discussion with Jake, but it's over now and we need to go to the restroom before class, if you'll excuse us."

I feel Amy and Jailene both staring at me as we breeze past her.

"I'm going to *kill* Peter," Jailene says. "I am going to *kill* him!"

"Jail!" Amy cries. "You think he really said all that? Jake is a liar!"

Jailene keeps walking. I wouldn't want to be Peter right now. I don't want to be me, either, but being Peter wouldn't be much better.

"Jailene!" Amy is practically screaming. Jailene stops to face her and backs her against the wall.

"What do you think, Amy? Think Jake would have the brains to make that up? I don't think he's that smart."

Yes, I think, yes, he is. But he wouldn't make that up. He's mean, but not that way. He has his own sense of justice, which is not lying. And now that I think about it, I've never known him to lie. The only time I thought he had lied was about the coyote, and that turned out to be the truth. That means he doesn't lie about what he plans to do, either, I realize, and that's not very comforting.

"You mean you *did* it?" Amy gapes. "Friday night with Peter? Oh, my God. Oh, my God, Jailene!"

"Shut up, okay?" Jailene says. "I'm going to the restroom." She hurries down the hall, leaving us to hold up the walls. I try hard to avoid Amy until the bell rings.

CHAPTER 15

Sometime during American studies, the sky lets loose a cold drizzle. I'm grateful that the rain will keep Dad from combining, so he'll be home in the barn doing chores with me tonight. Jake will stay away.

I go to the library during seventh-period study hall. I bury my nose in my novel in a study carrel to be alone where I can prop up my hand without being noticed. I want to curl up in a ball.

"I read that book." A voice comes over the wall of my cubicle. "I liked it."

I look up to see Arcadia looking over the wall at me.

"Oh, hi."

"What did you do to your hand?"

"I broke three bones."

"Obviously. I mean, how?" she says stepping around to where my chair is.

"Girls!" Ms. Parker, the librarian, barks, "This is a library."

Arcadia whispers, "Is that a boxer's fracture? Finger bones?"

"Um, I guess so." I feel my cheeks heat up and I look at my cast.

"Did you punch that Jake Riley kid that has a broken nose?"

Oh, God. If she's figured it out, everybody has.

"I'm sorry," she says, because she can see my panic, and I'm even more embarrassed. "I didn't mean to freak you out. I don't need to know. I didn't think it would be a big secret or anything."

My eyes hold hers, and I like her directness.

"It's"—I start to answer—"not so much a secret as it's that he'll be mad if everybody knows a girl broke his nose."

She grins, but before I can say anything else, Ms. Parker interrupts us. "Girls! Arcadia, take a seat. Now!"

"Later," Arcadia whispers and rolls her eyes. It always amazes me that Ms. Parker can be so intimidating although she probably weighs only ninety-eight pounds. But Arcadia sits.

I watch her settle in at a table behind me to do math. She grins at me again, almost shyly, then pulls out her calculator and buries her nose in her book. She's in advanced math, I notice: Geometry as a freshman, so she must be a brain.

I sit sort of sideways in my carrel with my hand propped up so I can watch her without being too obvious. Our eyes meet again several minutes later, and she smiles at me, as much with her dark brown eyes as with her mouth. She has a green stone in her nosering today. When the last bell rings, she waves to me, says, "See ya, Lainey," and disappears into the hall.

The rain is heavy by the time we get to the buses. I sit down right behind the driver to avoid Jake. I open my American studies book to try to keep from watching for him to get on. It takes lots of willpower not to look up and watch everybody climbing onboard. Either I look unfriendly or it's obvious that I want to be left alone, because nobody sits with me.

When everyone's finally on the bus, the driver winds up the engine for takeoff, coaxes the gearshift into first, and pulls out into the street.

I stare out into the rain, my cheek and nose pressed against the window. The glass is smooth and cold, and I wish I could press my tired, throbbing hand against it, but it's too awkward to prop my right hand up on my left side.

"Lainey-Belainey." I feel his breath on my neck the same instant I hear his voice. I jump so that the top of my cheek scrapes the bar across the middle of the bus window and my American studies book splats, pages down, on the wet bus floor.

I twist sideways to pick up the book with my left hand. I hold it in my lap with my cast and try to wipe the wet, brown grit from the slick pages with my left hand. "What do you want, Jake? Look what you did."

"Sorry, Lainey-Belainey."

"What *do* you want?" My heart is hammering, loud. Jake's never seen me scared of him before, but now I wonder if he can see my jacket pounding with my heart-beats. I tell myself it's because he surprised me, but my pounding heart isn't listening. I keep wiping at the wet pages, and I don't look at Jake.

He leans close to my shoulder, his chin on his hands on the back of my seat. One forearm rests against my back, so I lean forward to avoid the contact.

He speaks quietly, gently. "In Eldora, the guys who are sex offenders or minor offenders, they get treated like shit. I mean, the bigger guys do everything, *anything* to them. Nobody messes with the guys who're in for murder."

I keep wiping. I've rubbed half the print off these two pages now.

"Just wanted you to know why I'm gonna have to do it, Miss Smarty-Pants. It's not 'cause I hate you or nothin'. I just hafta do it." He leans back again, and I rest my head on the window, letting the textbook fall shut.

I hate the electricity in the air for the rest of the ride, and I can feel Jake's exact position behind me. I can feel his eyes shooting a hole in the back of my head.

The driveway has turned to mushy, gravelly mud, and I pick my way carefully, trying hard not to look to the road at Jake walking up his driveway. I can't let him know I'm scared.

I dress for chores, eat three peanut butter cookies, and swallow a glass of milk. Then Mom covers my cast in two plastic bread bags in an attempt to keep it clean and dry in the rain. The rubber bands just below my elbow pinch my skin. I pull on two old sweatshirts, and Mom slits the arm holes so they go over my cast. Dad said that tonight I have to feed the calves alone, one-handed. I was afraid to protest about how long it would take, but he must have read my mind because he said that it was just fine if it took me three hours because he guessed I needed to learn how to stay out of trouble. Hard work is his answer to everything.

Since I can only carry one bucket at a time now, I have to make four trips from the basement to the barn to carry all the warm water I need for the calf formula.

Dad's in the barn, messing with hog feeders in the far end past the shoot that stretches up into the silo. I set my buckets down inside the door, one at a time. It's slow going, mixing the formula and holding the buckets for all four little guys one-handed. At least they're growing so fast that they're tall enough to reach the nipple if I support the bucket on top of the fence with my good arm wrapped around it.

It takes every ounce of strength and courage that I have to pitch the dirty straw and manure from the calves' pen. I can hold the pitchfork handle with my left hand and rest it on my right forearm to give me leverage. It's pretty tiring to lift each forkful that way and dump it in the aisle where Dad can clean it with the Bobcat, especially with curious calves nosing me with every movement. By the time the pen is clean and I shake clean straw on their floor, my hand aches and I'm exhausted. I lean against their fence, rubbing their ears.

Dad comes down the aisle. "Not much fun to work one-handed, is it?" I shake my head and a drop of sweat flies with my hair. I hadn't even noticed I was sweating. He nods in understanding and goes down to start the Bobcat.

The Bobcat is a mini-tractor that is only as wide as its scoop so it can clean in tight places. It looks fun to run, but it's scary because it's balanced to lift heavy loads, and if the scoop is empty, it can flip backward or at least stand up on its back wheels like a rearing horse. I stand with my calves, watching Dad clear a widening path in the aisle.

"Lainey!" he yells over the motor. "Go feed the buck, will you? He's all that's left. Then we can go in."

"Okay." I throw my legs over the calf fence and go out to the sheep shed, which is a big Morton building extension off the north side of the barn. There are ewes in one half, late-market lambs that are living for the sole purpose of getting fatter for slaughter in the other half, and the black-faced Suffolk buck in a long narrow pen at one end of the shed. Dad calls him the Troll because he doesn't like anyone crossing his path. He'd as soon knock you over with his big head as look at you, and if you're carrying his bucket of feed, he'd rather knock you down and eat his food off the ground than let you dump it in his trough.

I can feed him in here, though, without getting into his pen. I toss him two slabs of hay from a broken bale, then I dump a quarter-bucket of cracked corn and half a coffee can of supplement over his fence. He bangs his head into the fence once to let me know who's boss before he starts to eat.

Dad shuts off the Bobcat just as I'm putting the bucket away. "Lainey! I'll take the calf buckets to the basement for you. Don't forget the light." I hear him pull the barn door shut. He's gone.

I hurry through the barn so I can get to the house, too. There's a noisy quiet in the barn, animals chewing and hunkering down for the evening with the drum of rain on the roof. It's a cozy place in the evening.

Suddenly the calm is split in two with the sharp crack of a rifle shot outside. I'm frozen for one step, then I'm screaming, running down the aisle. "Dad!" The animals jump and snort, startled, banging in their pens. "Dad!"

It's getting dark out. It's raining. Maybe Jake couldn't see who he was shooting at. Dad had his sweatshirt hood up, and he was carrying the calf buckets. I fumble one-handed with the latch on the barn door. I should have told Dad that Jake was in Eldora for *killing somebody*. I should have made him understand how dangerous the situation is. I thought I was saving myself by not telling Dad everything, but if I'd told him, he might have been more careful. I lift the latch and kick the door. It flies open. "Dad!" If Jake shot Dad, it's all my fault.

I can't see Dad anywhere, but Jake is standing by the crabapple tree, rifle in the crook of his arm, rain dripping from the brim of his baseball cap.

"Dad?"

No response.

"Jake, you bastard! What have you done?"

Jake nods toward the side of the barn. I run around the barn wall, letting the barn door swing behind me, and there's Dad, kneeling by the side of the barn. I feel as if I'm running in a slow-motion dream, trying to reach him. He looks up at me through the rain, shaking his head.

"Look, Lainey," he says, and then I see. There's a dead coyote in front of Dad, blood still streaming from its head just above the eye. The blood makes a dark puddle in the muddy grass.

"Dad." My breath rushes out in a relief.

"Lainey, what's the matter?" Dad stands and touches me on the shoulder. I'm fighting tears of relief.

"Good shot, son," he says.

Son! Son?

Dad hold his cap by the brim, slides it off, and scratches his head with the same hand. The rain runs in rivulets down his temples, and I feel it trickling down my neck, soaking my sweatshirts. My clothes are heavy, heavy. Dad shakes the rain out of his eyes and puts his cap back on, jamming it down on his wet hair.

"I reckon I owe you an apology, Jake. I didn't think the coyotes would come around here this time of year. Didn't believe you saw one. You did a good thing. However, it doesn't change the fact that you were forbidden to be over here and were trespassing to do it. Jake, you cannot be over here without your dad. Period. Understand?"

"Yes, sir."

I can't stand it. "I'm goin' in, Dad," I say.

Jake steps toward the dead coyote, grinning. His nose bandage is soaked, and falling off on one side, but he doesn't notice.

I go back and pick up the calf buckets that Dad set by the side of the barn, slinging two over my right arm. I latch the barn door shut and muck my way to the back door through the mud. Dad and Jake are dragging the dead coyote to the corncrib to skin it in the roofed alley where there's an electric light and they'll be out of the rain.

The pelt on a coyote is not worth anything, but the coyotes have been such a big problem for the turkey farmers in the last few years that the county pays a $15 bounty for each coyote killed. The pelt is taken as proof to collect the money.

I feel sick all over again. I rinse the buckets in the basement, then Mom meets me inside the back door.

"What's going on? What was that gunshot?"

"Jake killed a coyote. They're skinning it now."

"A coyote. Well, what do you know." She hands me a towel and I strip off my slippery bread bags and my wet clothes.

"Thanks," I say, wrapping the towel around my damp nakedness. I run upstairs and fill the bathtub with hot water and some bubbles, drop the towel, slide in, and prop my cast on the side of the tub.

I hate Jake for killing the coyote, for being right, for earning my dad's respect, for not lying. For not lying. A shiver runs through me in the hot water.

That means Peter really was bragging in the locker room, if I ever doubted it. Poor Jailene.

I let the steam rise around me and lift my knees, scalded red mountains in the white sea of bubbles.

This whole sex thing is so different than I thought it would be. One Christmas when I was in grade school, I asked Mom what the big deal was about a virgin getting pregnant, and she gave me a kid's book about sex. On the page where the married man and woman "love each other very much so they get as close as two people can be" in order to send the sperm on its way to the lucky little egg, the picture showed the husband and wife in bed, covered by a cozy homemade quilt.

Nothing, *nothing* that has happened in the last week has *anything* to do with that nice, homey picture.

I arch my back until my breasts protrude through the suds. I can almost make believe I have big boobs if I pile the bubbles around them just right. I think of Arcadia's tugboats. I wish I had breasts like that. But, then again, I wouldn't want to carry them around when I'm running.

I think of Jake looking at my breasts in the moonlight and I let them sink back under the suds. I wish that memory didn't stir my body the way it does. Like the stirring I feel when I watch sexy scenes in movies. So sex sure doesn't mean love. Love and sex can be two separate things. Stupid movies. They make us think once a couple has wrapped up in a big passionate embrace, everything will turn out okay. What a crock. The passionate embrace was the beginning of trouble for Jailene. And look how much trouble Jake has gotten into because of sex.

I rinse off the bubbles and hug a soft brown towel to my body.

Poor Jailene. A jerk has got her wrapped around his finger.

Poor me. A jerk has me in his rifle sights. I'm not sure which is worse.

CHAPTER 16

I hear Dad step down to the basement to wash. I imagine the coyote blood running in watery rivulets off his fingers and from the dark hair on his forearms. I wonder if Jake is back at his house, washing his own bloody hands, feeling fifteen dollars richer.

When Mom calls me to supper, we silently consume meatloaf and mashed potatoes and gravy. The quiet gets unbearable. Then Dad asks, "Why'd you scream tonight when you heard the gunshot, Lainey?" He takes another bite of meatloaf while he waits for me to reply.

"Dad, I thought Jake thought you were me. I thought he shot you, thinking he was killing me. The gun went off just as you went out of the barn, and I was sure he killed you."

"Hmm." Dad scoops some more mashed potatoes and gravy onto his plate.

"Dad, he's serious."

"He was after a coyote."

"Dad! Don't you get it? Why would he shoot the coyote just as you came out of the barn? If the coyote was running away, he had to have had a better shot at it when it was trying to get in the barn or something. I think he was sitting there with his twenty-two waiting for me, but when he saw you, he thought he better hurry up and kill the coyote or you'd see him with his gun without an excuse. I'm sure he was waiting for me! He was just lucky his coyote came along. That's why I went nuts when I heard the gunshot. I thought he shot you."

Mom wipes her mouth with her napkin. "I think, young lady, that your imagination has run away with you. How many times have you heard somebody say, 'I'll kill you, if you tell anybody'?"

"Mom! Jake was in the reform school for murder." There. It's out. They know. I set down my fork, watching their faces.

Dad narrows his eyes at me. "When did you find this out?"

"Friday night in the barn. When we fought and he said he'd kill me. He also said he'd kill me if I told you guys that he was in for killing somebody."

"His dad said he had been in for fighting," Dad says.

"Probably. Just the other guy died," I say.

"Who? How?" Mom asks.

"I have no idea. I didn't really want to ask, and I didn't want to spend any more time with him in the barn than I had to."

"I guess I'd better talk to Raymond," Dad says, pushing his plate away.

"Well, finish eating first," Mom says.

"Dad, if you go to Raymond, Jake will just find a way to kill me faster for telling you. You either have to send him back to Eldora or play it cool for a while. Please."

"I think we can set up some appropriate punishment," Dad says.

"Dad! Listen, cleaning the whole barn or something just isn't going to cut it this time. Please!"

The phone rings, interrupting us. It's Jailene.

"Can I call you back? We're in the middle of supper."

"Call me when you can really talk."

"It'll be after dishes and stuff."

"I don't care. Please."

Mom and Dad look at me with questions in their eyes. I don't usually make it obvious that I can't talk to one of my friends in front of them. I wish I had a phone in my room.

"Jailene," I say as I slip back into my chair and make an elaborate production out of cutting up my remaining meatloaf one-handed.

We eat quietly for a few minutes. My appetite is gone.

"Lainey, if Jake comes around our buildings again, he and Raymond are off the place," Dad says.

"*If* he comes again?" I ask. "*Again* will be too late."

Dad frowns and pushes back his plate. "I'll think of something, Lainey. Don't worry."

At least now, if I disappear, they'll know what happened. But I will worry.

Jailene calls me back before we're done with the dishes. I tell Mom I'll finish drying so I can have the kitchen to myself. Jailene is going nuts. "Laine, what if I'm pregnant?"

"Yeah. I thought of that. But, Jail, first time and all, what are the chances?"

"What if I'm pregnant and Jake kills you and I've got nobody but Amy?"

"Nice for you to be so concerned. But I guess that's the worst of our possibilities."

"Lainey, I'm sorry, but know what? If you're dead, you'd never have to worry about getting pregnant. I'd rather be dead than tell my dad I'm pregnant."

"Guess you have a point. But, Jail, you're not serious are you?"

"I wish Jake would shoot me instead of you."

"Don't talk like that. I need you around to help save me from him."

"I'll gladly jump in front of a bullet for you. Besides, if I'm big and pregnant, he couldn't miss."

"Jailene! You'd have a baby in there."

"I know what. If I'm pregnant, let's switch beds. Jake can shoot me through your bedroom window, so I won't have to tell my dad, and they won't have to deal with my suicide."

"And where will I be?"

"Tell you what. I'll do whatever I can for you with Jake, if you stick with me when Dad has disowned me and I have a huge swollen belly as big as a pufferfish and everybody at school looks at me like I'm a freak."

"Pufferfish are cute. I'm not exactly sure what you can do for me, but it's a deal."

We're quiet a moment, feeling the sweetness of friendship in spite of everything else. I put the last glass up in the cupboard. "Hey, have you talked to Peter?"

"No. But I know he's gonna call tonight. So I stayed

online, to keep the line busy and to give me time to figure out what to tell him."

"What do you want to tell him?"

"To go jump off a cliff."

"So tell him."

"What if I'm pregnant with his baby?"

"Tell him to jump faster and harder."

"What if Jake was lying and Peter's really sweet to me?"

"Jail, Jake doesn't—"

Jailene won't let me get a sentence in edgewise. "What if Peter really loves me?" she says.

"Do you love him?" I pull the plug and watch the dishwater spiral down the drain.

"I don't know. How are you supposed to know?"

"You're asking me? But, one thing, Jail: Jake never lies."

"What? You believe that?"

"I've been seeing it. The only time I ever thought he lied to me was when he said he saw a coyote by our barn. None of us believed him. Crazy Jake. Well, I saw one the other night, and tonight in the rain, Jake shot a coyote right outside the barn."

"Crap," Jailene says. "I hate him."

"Jake?"

"Peter."

"Oh. Yeah, me, too. Don't blame yourself."

"It's fun, but it's not worth this."

"I wouldn't know."

"The first part's wonderful. Touching and kissing. Laine, it's like your body can't contain the excitement and you can't get close enough, then all of a sudden, he can't stand it anymore, has to have you, and you're so turned on, you—"

Mom walks into the kitchen to get her new issue of *Country Home*.

"Just a minute!" I clamp my palm over the mouthpiece as if it will keep our conversation from spilling into Mom's ears.

"Lainey?" I can hear Jailene say from the receiver.

I try desperately to think of something to say to Mom, but I can't think of anything, so I give her a cheesy smile. I know my cheeks are red. She shakes her head and flips open her magazine as she steps out of the room.

"Okay," I say. "Mom was in here."

"Don't you ever get any privacy?"

"Go on."

"He wants to really do it, and you can hardly say no,

but you do, then he says that his ring means you're his, so it's okay, and he loves you and he's never felt like this before. Then it hurts like crazy, and later there's blood, just a little, and . . . oh, Lainey!" Jailene cries into the phone.

For a second, I think I can feel the tears coming out of the holes in my receiver, then I realize I'm holding it so tight I'm sweating.

"I was in love on Friday night. And I loved it. Now I hate him. I can't believe I did it. I wish I could do Friday night all over again. I keep waiting to wake up and have it be a bad dream. Lainey, I'm a horrible person."

"Why?"

"Because I liked it so much. All but the last part."

"Jail, I don't think it's bad to like it. I think it's probably normal. But what do I know?"

"You know, Lainey, I'd be crazy in love with him right now if he'd have stopped when I asked him to . . . or even if he hadn't gone bragging in the locker room! Holy goddamn buckets, I hate him for that. I hate him! What if I go to hell for having sex with somebody I hate? And my dad will kill me if he ever finds out—like if I'm pregnant—so I might go soon."

"Hell? You're not serious, are you? About believing in hell?"

"Yeah."

"I'd say your dad killing you is hell enough. You've got enough to worry about without worrying about going to hell. Anyway, you'll be in good company. I'll be there before you, if Jake gets me."

"Great. Maybe you'll get a private phone down there."

We laugh. It's nervous at first, but we can't stop laughing, it feels so good.

"Well," she says through her giggles, "thanks for making me laugh."

"Oh, Jail. I told Mom and Dad why Jake was in Eldora, so they'd take me seriously."

"Good! I feel better about you. A teeny-tiny bit."

"Thanks for calling. I don't know what else to say."

"Say good night. I've got to talk to Peter. You know, it might have felt a lot different if he couldn't wait to see me this morning. If he came to my locker. But no, he couldn't wait to go brag in the locker room. I hate him! I never saw him all day. For the first time since he asked me out. What a jerk."

"Good luck. Hey," I ask as a last thought, "did you use a condom? How scared are you about being pregnant?"

"Yeah we used one. He had one in his pocket. Which

makes me mad now, too, knowing he was planning on doing it."

"Oh, jeez. But you should be safe then, shouldn't you? I think you have enough to worry about. Don't think about the pregnancy thing yet, unless ya have to, okay?"

"Okay. Night, Lainey."

If I weren't sure that Jake was serious, I would think I was the lucky one.

CHAPTER 17

When the bus pulls up to the school the next morning, Arcadia is leaning against one of the beams under the front overhang, out of the still-falling rain, looking as if she's expecting someone.

I get off the bus, trying to keep my cast dry, and Arcadia steps down to the sidewalk to meet me.

"Hi."

"Hi." I wonder if my face shows her how surprised I am that it was me she was waiting for.

I wait for her to say something, but she just walks beside me as if we've done this every morning since kindergarten. When we turn into the hall where our lockers are and the crowd is thick, she says, "Jake was in Eldora, wasn't he?"

I turn to face her so abruptly that my backpack flies down from my shoulder and bangs into her arm.

"I'm sorry," I say.

She laughs and shoves the strap up where it was on my left shoulder.

As we make our way down the hall, I ask, "How did you know?"

"You hang around those guys enough, you can pick them out."

"Those guys? In reform school?"

"Yeah. Actually, my dad used to be the chaplain in Eldora."

"In Eldora? The chaplain? Your *dad?*"

"Yeah. Yeah, and yeah. Actually, it's called a treatment center, not a reform school anymore. More PC, you know. It's now the Eldora Adolescent Treatment Facility. And, yes, I'm a preacher's kid. I look like it, don't I?" In the middle of the crowded hall, she twirls around so her dyed black hair and her short, black, crocheted dress twirl out, and you can see her leggings up to her butt. She looks like a druggie, not a preacher's kid.

"I always thought there was something familiar about Jake, but I didn't give it much thought until when you and your friends had that altercation with him by the steps yesterday. Then I remembered him from when I used to visit Dad at work."

I glance at her body. "I bet the boys liked that! So what do you remember about him?"

"Nothing more than his face. The look he had when Amy rushed him brought it back. He doesn't smoke anymore, does he?"

"N-no. I don't think so."

"Amazing. That he quit, I mean. Everybody in there smokes; it's a rite of passage. I don't know anybody else who started in there and quit. He must have some moral fortitude."

"Huh. *Moral fortitude* is not exactly the way most people would describe him."

She laughs again. She laughs like she dances, with strength and grace. Her teeth are as strong and white as her body is strong and lean. "Would you?"

"What?"

"Describe him that way?"

"Um, well, he never lies, and he's got guts and determination, and he has a strong sense of justice. It's a very warped sense of justice, but he sticks to what he believes. So, no, not really, but yes in some ways."

"Why'd you punch him? Are you friends with him?"

I stop to look her in the eye, and the kid walking behind me rams into my backpack. We keep moving.

"Not anymore. We used to be. He's my neighbor. Now I hate him. He's perverted."

"Obsessed with sex?"

"Huh?" I'm so startled by her question that I hardly know what to say, but I hurry to answer so she won't think I don't understand what she means. "Yeah. Yeah! How did you know?"

"They're all obsessed with it. In my dad's opinion, God got confused when He put together males between the ages of thirteen and twenty. He transposed two letters in the directions and the brain got put where the groin was supposed to be."

We hoot at this, and I say, "A pastor said that?"

She smiles. "My dad's cool. Except it's not very easy to convince him to let me out on a date when he holds that theory."

I grin at her while she keeps talking.

"I think I agree with him that all teenage boys are obsessed with sex. Probably all teenage people." She smiles. "But in a treatment center, it's like everything is magnified, so it's truer than ever. And worse, the teenage boys who have lived in a closed setting like that don't know that it's not socially acceptable to make the fact public."

"Sounds like Jake."

"My dad says that most teenage boys think they're the only ones in the world that masturbate every night, and they're all ashamed to tell anybody else. In reform school, I mean in a treatment center, there's no privacy, so they all know everybody else masturbates, too. They're all obsessed, so nobody's embarrassed, and they forget it's something that is usually a secret or at least private. They have no clue what the word *restraint* means. Dad used to say he was on his way to work at the 'hormone dorm.'"

"Ha." I think about what Jake said about the boys there. We're walking as slowly as we can down the hall, and we dodge a few more shoulders on our way.

"So, why'd you punch him?"

"He says he'll kill me, if I tell."

"Does he mean it?"

I nod.

"Wow. So what are you going to do?"

"I sure wish I knew."

"There are teenage murderers in there, in Eldora, you know."

"Yeah, I know. And he says he'd rather go in for murder than for anything else. Says if I tell what he did, he'll have to go back, that he'll have to kill me so he won't be going back for anything but murder."

"That's messed up. But, tell what? What did he do?"

"Lainey!" Jailene's voice breaks into our private connection. "I thought you'd never get here." Jailene pushes her way through the hall to me, and then she sees who I'm talking to and says, "Oh, hi, Arcadia."

"Hi, Jailene. See you seventh period, Elaine?"

Nobody my age calls me Elaine. I hated the name until this very moment. "Yeah. I'll talk to you then. Bye."

Arcadia touches my shoulder and is gone.

"Elaine?" Jailene asks. "She calls you Elaine?"

I shrug. "What happened when Peter called?"

"Come here." She grabs my elbow and drags me around the corner where it's not so crowded. "Listen, Laine. Peter called the minute I hung up with you last night," Jailene buzzes.

"And?"

"I asked him what he'd do if I'm pregnant."

"And?"

"He said, 'I can tell it was your first time, if you're so worried about that,' but he's sure I'm not. And I said, 'Why? Are you sure you shoot blanks?' He got really mad at me, and finally he said if I was, he guessed he'd make sure I got an abortion, and if I didn't get one, it would be my problem, not his. But that it was really *immature* to worry about that when we'd used a condom."

"Jeez. Nice guy."

"Then he said I should thank him for bringing protection, and I said he shouldn't have assumed that was going to happen, and I wasn't exactly expecting to do what we did. Then we both yelled at each other, and I said I couldn't believe he bragged in the locker room that we'd done it and I hated him and never wanted to see him again, and if I was pregnant, I was going to show up on his mom's doorstep and ask her advice."

"Jeez!"

"He started swearing at me and said it was none of his mom's business. And I said he should have thought of whose business it was when he made it everybody's business in the locker room. He said he did no such thing, but he didn't sound very convincing, and I said I heard it from a reliable source. He didn't have much else to say, and we hung up on each other at about the same time."

"A reliable source? Jake?"

"You said he didn't lie."

"He doesn't. And he has some moral fortitude."

"What are you talking about? The guy is trying to kill you, and you say he's got *moral fortitude*? Are you nuts?"

"Never mind. So how are you now?"

"I wish I were dead." We lean against the wall. "It's

hard to remember why I liked him so much."

Meredith Baker and her clones giggle past. For a moment, I wish our lives were as simple as it looks like hers is.

"It was because he's cute and popular, has a great laugh and a great butt . . ." I remind her.

"Yeah. And that's not all, either!"

"Jail!" I squeal at her and smack her shoulder with my left hand. "Care to elaborate on that?"

She tries to laugh through the tears that are squeezing out, and she fishes a Kleenex out of her jeans pocket to blow her nose. Peter's ring comes flying out with the Kleenex, and the ring goes bouncing across the floor among a hundred sandals and Nikes and Reeboks. "Shoot," she says.

We chase the ring and battle bodies and book bags across the hall until I spy it by the lockers. We're follow it spinning along until a Nike toe lifts and stops the ring under its sole. Jailene bends to pick it up, but the toe doesn't move. She looks up into Jake's eyes.

"Oh. Hi, Jake. Thanks," she says.

"Hi, Jailene." He looks at me as he crouches to pick it up. "Look," he says, holding it up. "The ring of Peter the Great. This ring must have some power over whoever wears it."

Jailene cringes and reaches for the ring.

Jake lifts it out of her reach and says, "By the way, Peter the Great said nice things about you yesterday, too."

Jailene stops, frozen. Jake lowers the ring until both their fingers hold it. I watch pain and hope cross Jailene's red cheeks. I hope she's not a sucker for sweet talk.

"He said you were great. Beautiful knockers. Real sexy."

Jailene snatches the ring from him, and in one big circular movement, she swipes him across the face with the hand holding the ring.

We both gasp as we see a deep scratch from the ring bloom in a neat line of blood across his cheek. He grabs his cheek. "Shit! Get the hell away from me! Both of ya," he growls and heads for the bathroom.

"What an asshole! You know, I didn't mean to make him bleed," Jailene says, "but I'm not a bit sorry."

"I rest my case," I say, holding up my cast.

She grins and slides her arm around my shoulder.

"You know what Arcadia said this morning?"

She shakes her head.

"That all boys have their brains where their groins are supposed to be. The ones who have been in reform school don't know how to hide it."

"I know one who hasn't been in reform school who thinks with his groin and forgot to keep it a secret. By the way, if he's so eager to have his you-know-what inside something, maybe I should stuff it inside this." She holds up the ring.

We laugh. It feels good to laugh with Jailene this morning. I'm not going to try to explain that Jake didn't have a clue that he was totally out of line, insulting. It was insulting, and that's what matters to Jailene. We go to class.

Mr. Eikton gives us another creative writing assignment. We're supposed to write about the thing in our lives that has made us the angriest. We're supposed to write about what we saw and did but never mention the words *anger, mad, rage, furious*, or any other feeling word. We're supposed to *show* the emotion. I start writing.

I didn't stop to think. I just let my fist fly and felt the crack of the bones in my hand and the snap of his nose. That wasn't enough. I wanted to kick and kick and kick and kick until he was a bloody pulp and I could shovel him out with the manure. I had to help him out of the barn, of course, and then Mom felt sorry for him and took him to the hospital even though I was sitting in the house with broken bones, too. I threw up and threw up. I think I was throwing up what he did.

I write really slowly with my left hand so that's all I've written when Mr. Eikton starts wandering around the room to read over our shoulders and offer advice.

"This is good, Meredith," he says to Meredith Baker, who is clad in skin-tight pants and a clingy Slater Danceline T-shirt. "But don't use the word *hate*, either. It's an emotive word that doesn't show the feelings—it tells us what to feel."

He wanders on toward my desk and I am panicky. I feel the sweat trickle down my back. I have shown emotion clearly here without saying what made me mad, but I don't dare let Mr. Eikton see this. I've spread the word that I smashed my hand in the barn. I weight the spiral notebook with my cast and start to rip out the page with my left hand. I can tell Eikton that I drew a blank. Writer's block. Can't let him see this. He'll ask too many questions. The page scrunches, ripping, but not from the spiral. Out of the corner of my eye I see Eikton's pants.

Right beside me.

"May I see, Lainey?"

I munch the page up with my left hand, trying to pull it in a wad from the spiral, and shake my head. "It's no good."

"Let me be the judge of that. You don't have time to start over and still get credit for this exercise."

I hold the crumpled paper, moving it away from him. This reminds me of the time my fourth-grade teacher put tape on my mouth: Just as the tape got to my lips, I'd open my mouth and foil her again and again until she was so mad I thought she'd smack me, so I finally held my lips together for her. I relinquish the paper and slide my head into my hand. I'm dead.

"This is good, Lainey, very good," Mr. Eikton says. "It shows emotion instead of telling. Want to turn it in as it is?"

"No!" I say too quickly.

The whole class is looking at me and my cheeks are burning.

"Here." Mr. Eikton hands it back to me. "I'd turn it in for credit if I were you. See me after class."

After class, Mr. Eikton looks at me the same way he did after the squirrel incident. "Yours was the best piece in class. Why didn't you want to turn it in?"

I hang my head and shrug. "I—I just didn't mean to write that. I shouldn't have. It's private. Please?"

"Why did you write it down then?"

"'Cause you said to write about the thing that made us the angriest, and this was it."

"Talk to me, Lainey. What's going on?"

"I don't want you to show it to anybody else, and I've been saying that I smashed my hand in the barn, which is true. But everybody doesn't need to know that I smashed it against someone's face in the barn."

Mr. Eikton nods. "Care to tell me why?"

I shake my head. "I can't."

"Tell you what. It'll be between you and me, if you take it home and write it—the whole scene. If it's as good as the first part, it means an A on this assignment. And I won't show anyone. You have my word." He smiles. "Unless, of course, something went on that is illegal. Then I'm required by law to report it." I swallow so hard I can hear the lump in my throat go down. "And even if you don't want to write about it, maybe you ought to talk to somebody about what happened. Think about it, Lainey. See you tomorrow," he says.

I nod dumbly and stumble out the door. If I'm alive, you'll see me tomorrow.

CHAPTER 18

The rain keeps drizzling down. By noon, I'm relieved—
even if it stops raining, the ground will be too soggy for
Dad to take the combine out in the field. That gives me
one more night with him in the barn. I should be pray-
ing that it rains from now 'til April.

When Arcadia slides into the seat at the table next
to me in the library during seventh period, I don't greet
her very enthusiastically. I'm scared that Jake will recognize her if he sees us together. I'm scared that I've
already said too much to her. I don't even know her. But
part of me hopes maybe, just maybe, she'll know how to
help me send him back. That's why I sat at a table
instead of a study carrel in hopes that I could talk to her.
I'm paying, though. There's no place to prop my hand
and by this time in the day, it's throbbing. I set my elbow
on the table and hold my hand upright.

"*Now* what happened to Jake?" she whispers. The librarian is not far away.

"What do you mean?"

"Not only does he have a taped nose and two black and blue eyes, but now he has a long scratch running across his cheek. Looks fresh. He's in bad shape."

I can't help grinning. "He made a very inappropriate remark and Jailene backhanded him."

Arcadia smiles. "Let me take a wild guess. Some sexual comment?"

I nod.

"Maybe I like that Jailene after all. I wasn't too impressed with her at the dance, but she seems okay." That makes me smile, to think of getting a first impression of Jailene by watching her plastered against Peter.

"It was a bad night for her." I have no intention of saying too much about Jailene, so I add, "I think she was acting a little out of character. Wasn't too happy with herself later."

Arcadia smiles. "I wouldn't mind stepping out of character with the right person. Brad Pitt, perhaps . . ."

We both giggle, and we stick our noses in our books until we've stopped shaking.

"So, what's new with you?" she asks. "What was all that about in English? What's happening with Jake?"

"He shot a coyote last night."

"What?"

I tell her the whole story about thinking Jake was lying, Dad banishing him from our barnyard, finding out after the dance that he wasn't lying, and scaring me to death last night when I thought he shot Dad.

"Good grief. So part of what he did is trespass, right?"

"Yeah."

"Does your father believe that Jake is making a serious threat? To kill you, I mean?"

"Sometimes I think so, but mostly I think not. I'm sure I'll come home some night and Jake will be cleaning the whole barn with a pitchfork as punishment. Work is Dad's answer to everything. But it'll be lots worse if Jake knows I told Dad everything and he doesn't get sent back to Eldora. Is trespassing enough to send him back?"

"No, I don't think so. What else did he do?"

I sigh, then I hand her the crumpled-up essay from Eikton's class. Midway through reading it, she looks me straight in the face and whispers, "What did Jake do?"

I shake my head. "Can't tell you. Not here and now, anyway," I whisper back. "But Eikton says I have to finish it and turn it in tomorrow if I want the grade, showing the whole scene—why I was so angry. As if I'd trust him with that information after what he did with my poems."

"Which was what?" Arcadia asks, finishing the short page. "You write well, by the way. I mean, *how* you write. Your penmanship is lousy."

"Thanks, I think. Eikton took a poem I wrote about Jake to Prebyl!"

"Prebyl the stone woman? Someone ought to crack her plaster face with a hammer . . . or we could take chisels and carve another Mount Rushmore in the makeup on her face without touching skin!" We hide behind our books again, shaking with laughter. When I look up, Ms. Parker is giving us a look to kill.

We actually study for awhile so we won't get kicked out of the library entirely.

Finally, Ms. Parker goes behind a row of stacks, and Arcadia whispers, "What did Prebyl do with the poem?"

"Called me into her office and said she was concerned about my *relationship* with Jake."

"And what did you tell her?"

"As little as possible. Almost nothing."

I tell Arcadia about the squirrel, too. She says, "You can't write that essay for Eikton after all that, can you?"

"I've got an A if I do."

"I think your life is a tad more important than one grade, don't you? Write something else. It shouldn't be too tough to think of another time you were really pissed off."

I grin at her. "You don't exactly talk like a pastor's kid."

"God, I hope not." We smile. "Hey!" she says. "Maybe . . . God, I wish we had a different counselor than Mrs. Pebble."

I chuckle. "Why?"

"Because a counselor is supposed to help. If you did this right, your essay could send him back to Eldora. This might be your lifesaver."

I bite my lip, not very willing to buy into this.

"Did he do anything that would send him back? Anything illegal? Can you tell me that much? Sexual assault would count."

"I'm thinking . . . Eikton said that what I wrote would be between him and me—unless Jake did something illegal. So I either have to write something totally different and play it safe, or I have to spell it all out."

Arcadia nods. "Looks like it."

"How do I know if it was illegal?"

"What did he do?"

"Well, that's twice now that he's shot a gun in our

barnyard, once after being ordered never to be on the place without his father. That's something. He's sexually harassed me, made advances, grabbed at me."

"That why you punched him?"

"No. I always got away before." Ms. Parker goes out of sight into the back of the room. "Okay, here's what happened," I whisper. "Friday night after the dance, I heard noise in the barn and went out to check on my calves."

"As in baby cows, as opposed to the muscles in your legs?" I raise my eyebrows at her, and she shrugs. "Just checking," she says, smiling. "Go on about the baby cows."

"And Jake was in their pen. He didn't see me come in, so I sort of sneaked closer. When he did see me, he quickly zipped up his jeans."

"Yuck! What was he doing?"

"I don't know, but he said if I told, he'd kill me."

"But you've already told, right? Your parents know?"

"Yeah."

"So when did you break his nose?"

"I called him a perverted piece of slime and he came at me and I punched him—punched him in the stomach, too. First I thought he meant he'd kill me if I told anyone that I beat him up, but he meant that he didn't want me to tell whatever he was doing."

"Whew."

"And then he told me that he'd rather go back to Eldora for murder than for anything else, so if I told, he'd have to kill me so he'd have respect in there."

Arcadia nods. "Anything else?"

"He told me . . ." I'm suddenly scared I've said way too much to too many people, and this is out of my control.

Arcadia watches my face, waits.

There's no going back now. "He said he was in for murder before, so he won't have any problem doing it again."

"Wow." She sighs. "That's pretty serious stuff. I think if Prebyl knew all that, she would do anything she could to put him away."

"Oh, my gosh, Arcadia. I just remembered. Jake said he saw part of his file in her office, and it said he was irreparably damaged. She must already know why he was in there. I never thought of that. She's just looking for an excuse to expel him."

"Good Lord. That's enough to make me not want him to go back. Except to keep you safe, of course. I thought counselors were supposed to believe in their students when nobody else did. Do you think he's irreparable?"

"I do now, 'cause I'm scared. I didn't before. But now I hate him, 'cause of all the stuff he's done."

She nods. "I can see that. But I'm afraid, Elaine, that you may hold Jake's life in your hands."

"Well, he's got mine in the sights of his rifle."

"And you have his at the point of your pen."

"Oh, great. Advantage: Jake Riley."

"Maybe not. The pen is more powerful than—"

"A sword, not a rifle."

We smile. "Another thing," she says, "is that you'll give the Pebble woman a lot of satisfaction if you let her crush him."

"That's the one thing that could change my mind about this essay," I say. "I don't want her to be right."

"Girls!" We've passed Ms. Parker's tolerance level and have pushed her into a mild rage. "If you have this much to talk about, take it to study hall. You don't belong in the library today. I've given you enough chances. Go. Now." She scribbles out hall passes for us.

We take them, trying to keep our faces straight, and as soon as we're in the hall, we double up with laughter.

"Oops. I forgot entirely where we were!"

We laugh all the way to the lunchroom, where seventh-period study hall is held, and where not one person is studying. There are hubs of conversation and laughter spread throughout the room. It shouldn't even be called study hall. We slide over to a deserted table and look at each other.

"So what should I do?" I ask.

"I don't know. Want to come stay at my house a few days to be safe while you consider it?"

"I don't have a few days. I have to decide today. Besides I hardly know you. Your mom would freak out, wouldn't she? Bringing home a strange girl who's hiding out from a psycho who wants to kill her?"

"You're not so strange." She grins. I wrinkle my nose at her. "Actually, she's been a pastor's wife, you know. She's fed transients before."

"Thanks a lot. What about your dad?"

"You won't see him. They're divorced. That's why we moved here. And Dad took a chaplaincy in Washington, D.C., so I'll only see him in the summer and holidays and stuff."

"I'm sorry. Wow, you're not the typical pastor's family, are you?"

"Hardly. So you *could* come home with me. Mom would be glad if I made a friend here."

I feel bad for her. "You know, I'd like to, but I have to go home and feed my calves."

"Can't somebody else do that?"

"No. They're my responsibility. That was the deal when Dad got them for me. But it's more than that: They're my babies. They need me, and if I'm not there, what do you think Jake might do to them?"

"So you protect them one-handed?"

"Yeah. It's a treat. But I don't have a choice."

"What will you do, one-handed, if he comes after you?"

"I don't have a clue."

"Well, get a plan before you go to the barn alone, okay? Call me, would you, so I know if you're okay tonight?" She scribbles her number, four inches high across a notebook page, and stuffs it in my backpack. "Don't forget. I'll worry."

CHAPTER 19

Jake doesn't speak to me on the bus. The scratch on his cheek has crusted over, and he seems sullen. I take that as a bad sign. He's not even teasing me anymore.

I press my forehead against the bus window and thank God for the drizzle that's still falling. Thinking of God, it still amazes me that Arcadia is a pastor's daughter.

Mom's outside, so I call Jailene as soon as I get off the bus. I didn't see her all afternoon, and I want to check in and update her on Arcadia, but the line's busy. She's always online. I change clothes and try again. It's still busy, so, feeling very much alone, I put a bag over my cast and head for the basement.

I hurry to chore while Dad's in the barn. I feed the babies and feed the Troll without being asked. He hits the gate so hard while I'm leaning against it that he almost knocks me over. I don't want Dad to spring any last-minute jobs on me. More and more, my calves are mouthing the solid food that I pour into their trough from the striped Supersweet bag. When they eat it really well, I won't nipple feed them anymore. That will be a lot easier, but I'll miss feeling needed this way.

Dad and I walk back to the house together. He has two of my buckets. There's been no sign of Jake. Dad says the rain is supposed to stop tonight. I sigh.

During supper, Jailene calls to say that Peter has not called her, and he is the jerk of the century. I agree and make sure that Mom and Dad see that I'm not afraid to talk in front of them.

"What was the big deal about the essay in Eikton's class?" Jailene asks.

I tell her.

"Well, you're not going to write it, are you? Are you nuts?"

"I'll call you back."

After supper, I call and tell her about my conversation with Arcadia.

"Are you sure you're ready to do that? Put Jake *away*, I mean? I know you hate him—we all hate him—but if you do it, there's no going back."

I finally sit down to write. I try for forty-five minutes

to write something else. I write about being mad at Amy for revealing my secret, but it doesn't work, mostly because I'm afraid she'll read it. Finally, I write about getting my mouth taped shut in fourth grade, and how mad I was at my teacher and how embarrassed because the principal walked in while I sat there, my mouth taped shut; I had opened my desk to hide my face from him.

It's a bad essay, and it's only three-fourths of a page, but my left hand can't take any more than that. I could use the computer, but then Eikton would expect it to be even better.

I finally curl up in bed to read, right hand propped on three pillows, hoping it will distract me.

It takes a long, long time to fall asleep. I dream that Jake is sitting on the roof of our front porch, pointing his gun through my bedroom window at me. He says, "Sorry I have to kill you, Lainey-Belainey, but you don't understand what it's like." Just as he pulls the trigger, I wake up screaming and sweaty.

It's dark outside and my clock reads 4:50. I tiptoe to my window. The porch roof right under my window is empty. There's a noise by the drainpipe. It rattles with the weight of something, and I know why people use the expression "My blood ran cold." That's how it feels. I move back toward my bed slowly, like in the dream, and stuff two of the pillows under my blankets to look as if I'm in bed there. Then I open my bedroom door for a fast escape before I get down on my hands and knees and crawl back to the window for a better look, wincing from the pain in my right hand.

The rain has stopped, but a cold breeze sifts through the storm window and the drainpipe rattles hard. I can see it shake. Something comes up over the edge of the roof. It's brown. It looks like a hand in a leather glove, and I'm out of my bedroom and flying down the steps in four jumps.

I land smack at the bottom against Dad, who grabs my good arm.

"What's going on?" he asks. "I heard you scream."

I start to say that it was a dream, but no words come out. "Shh," I say. I grab him by the hand and hold tight, waiting for a gunshot at the top of the stairs. It doesn't come. On tiptoe, I pull Dad up the steps to my room, and we peer around the curtain to the window. On the roof sits a fat squirrel, in the darkness, nibbling on the stump of an ear of corn, chattering quietly to himself.

"A squirrel?" Dad asks. The squirrel hears him and freezes.

"I thought . . ." I feel myself deflate.

My sigh is loud enough to send the squirrel fleeing, and as he turns, he drops the corncob remainder, and we see that he has only three legs.

"Well, I'll be dad-burned," Dad says.

"It worked," I say. "He's alive."

"Lucky little son of a gun," Dad says.

"I screamed because of a dream," I say, "and then I heard something on the roof, and I thought . . ."

"You thought it was Jake."

I nod against Dad's shoulder.

He pats my head like he did when I was a little girl. "Your imagination is working overtime. I don't think you need to be quite so terrified about his threat. You know how to take care of yourself."

"Dad, he said he'd shoot me through my window some night when I'm sleeping. There's no way to take care of yourself against that."

"But it was a squirrel after all. In fact, it was *the* squirrel you two saved. Now, think about that and go back to sleep." He pats my shoulder, turns, and his feet thump descending notes down the stairs. I sink back into my bed.

Forty-five minutes later, still wide awake, I get up and get ready to feed the calves. When I'm done and walking back to the house, the sun is peeking over the horizon through a freshly washed, clear blue sky that's reflected in a hundred mud puddles in the barnyard.

On the bus the next morning, Jake looks awful. His nose is freshly taped, so it's all the more obvious, all pure white and clean. The scratch from Peter's ring on his cheek is pink and raised. I wonder if it's infected.

"Jake," I say. I want to tell him about the squirrel, as a sort of peace offering, but he doesn't look at me. He has dark circles under his eyes as if he didn't sleep at all last night. I wonder what he was doing. I don't want to know. I wish I hadn't finished my book, so I'd have a way to distract myself.

Eikton strolls up and down the desks, collecting essays from the few of us who took them home to finish last night. Mine is lying on the top of my desk, face-down. I'm so glad I didn't write about Jake. I'm safe for another few hours. Eikton holds out his hand for my paper, reads the first sentence, and frowns before he moves to the next desk.

I'm in art, trying to use my left hand to draw yet another still life. This one is two candles and some silk cloth piled around artificially. If I had my right hand, it would be easier to draw than the fruit was, but nothing's easy this way.

"Peter called last night after I talked to you," Jailene says.

"And?" I respond, straining with my pencil.

"He asked me to go to a movie with him on Friday."

"Is this guy brain-dead or what?"

"I said yes."

"You what?" My pencil stops and I whirl toward her.

"He said he was *really* sorry he was such a jerk and if I'm *really* pregnant, of course he'll *really* help me get an abortion, and he *really* wants to see me again," she whispers.

"*Really?*"

Jailene nods. Sometimes she doesn't listen to herself and she doesn't get the joke.

"He says he can't stop thinking about me."

"*Really?* Well, I'll kick him in the nuts for you if you want me to. Might force you out of his mind for a few minutes."

She giggles, but when she realizes I'm serious, she turns red. "At least I don't have anybody trying to kill me."

"*Destroying* you doesn't count, I guess, like killing you on the inside? Or what about—if you should just happen to be pregnant, which you probably aren't—

being willing to kill the baby?"

"Lainey!"

Ooh. That was nasty of me. I shouldn't have said that, but I see it on her face too late. Jailene puts her hand up to cover her eyes.

"Jail, I'm sorry. I didn't mean it. Well, not all of it, anyway. It's just that I can't forgive him for talking about you like that in the locker room. I hate him for how he's treating you."

She doesn't look up. "He said he was sorry."

"*Really* sorry, you mean."

"He said—" She stops midsentence, realizing that I'm making fun of Peter's conversation with her. She rolls her eyes, trying not to stay serious. "Lainey, he said on the phone that he realizes . . . that he loves me. And he's rea—" She stops herself from saying it. "That he's sorry."

"He's *sorry*? Sorry for making you sound like a slut? Jail, that doesn't sound like love. I think he's just horny again and wants you again. Think about it, Jail."

She turns slightly away from me on her art stool.

"Jail."

She says nothing.

"Jail, I'm sorry, but you said yourself he thinks with his groin."

"I like him, okay?"

"Fine. But two nights ago, you couldn't remember what you'd ever seen in him. Remember?" I don't know what else to say to her. Love is blind. Man, is that true. Dear God, I hope I'm never like that.

While I imagine ways to build the bridge back to Jailene that I just destroyed, I get the candle outlined. I'm trying to get the shape of the silk right before I start shading when the classroom door opens.

Mrs. Prebyl's head enters, followed by a powder blue dress with a million tiny accordion pleats in the skirt. It swirls out from her hips, and it looks like she's wearing a circus tent attached to her waist. It doesn't do anything but exaggerate her large hips. Her eyes scan the room, and I bend my head and work furiously. She whispers something to Mr. Reed.

"Elaine?" Mr. Reed says. "Would you please come here? You can put your supplies away."

"But I need time to draw," I say. "I'm slow with my left hand."

"Mrs. Prebyl wants to see you."

"Ooh. Now what?" some wiseass from the back of the room says.

"I don't want to see her," I murmur under my breath.

Jailene stares at me in horror. The words came out louder than I thought they did. Soft laughter ripples around the room.

"I'd rather be you," I whisper to Jailene as I sign the beginnings of my picture and put it and my drawing pencil away. "At least you have some choices."

As I turn to follow Mrs. Prebyl out the door, Jailene grabs my good wrist and whispers, "So do you. You can tell them everything and send him away, you know. *Now.*"

Mrs. Prebyl says nothing on the way down the hall. She knows better than to try to make small talk. She closets us in her office, pulls a folder from a drawer, and lays my essay on the top of her desk. Somehow, Mr. Eikton has betrayed me, and I didn't even give him any ammunition. I swallow.

"Mr. Eikton informed me that yesterday you wrote the beginnings of a powerful essay about punching someone in the nose, and he told you to finish the essay, to tell why you punched whoever it was."

I nod, trying to look relaxed, but there's sweat in my armpits.

"He said that whatever you wrote would be between

him and you unless it was something he legally had to report."

I nod again, and the sweat trickles down my ribs.

"So what do you have to say for yourself?"

"Nothing. There's nothing to say. I wrote something else—about getting mad in fourth grade."

"Exactly the point. We're not stupid, Elaine. You didn't finish your essay about punching someone because we're sure that would mean we would have something to report—that the someone you punched did something illegal. Elaine, you're—"

"Please call me Lainey."

"You're an honor student, and Jake has a history of trouble. To write such a poor essay when Mr. Eikton said your other one was outstanding—some of the best writing he's seen—only adds up to the fact that you must be hiding something Jake has done. It doesn't take many brains to figure out that you broke your hand punching Jake in the nose. We can't help him if you don't tell us what it was he did."

"Help him? You don't want to help him! You don't think he can be helped, do you? Your file on him says *irreparably damaged*. You just want to send him away so you don't have the problem kid in *your* school and *you* won't have to deal with him anymore."

"Elaine. *Lainey*." She says the word as if it doesn't fit in her mouth. "We're concerned about the safety of all our students. If one student puts others at risk, we are obligated to remove him."

"How would you get him removed?" I ask.

"We'd follow the proper legal channels, of course. It might take a few weeks, most likely, unless he's an immediate threat to someone. But Elaine—*Lainey*— you must know, it doesn't help anyone if you keep trying to protect him."

"I'm not . . ." I jump up from the chair, and I'm out the door before she can say anything but "Elaine, wait!"

I don't have a plan until I'm in the hall. I run, and I can hear Mrs. Prebyl's high heels clicking after me in a stilted trot. As she chases me down the hall, I wonder how those spindly little heels can support all her weight. "Elaine!" she calls out, trying to sound full of an authority she'll never have.

I stop at Mr. Eikton's door and pull it open without knocking. He's in full session with his class. I stare at him and our eyes meet. "Can I see you, please?" I ask.

"Can it wait? I'm in the middle of class."

"No, it can't."

"Please, Elaine."

"It's Lainey. Or did you forget that, too?"

He steps toward me. "Um, class, I want you to read the rest of that passage and write two sentences about what you think it means for the main characters." He steps to the door and says quietly, "What is it, Lainey? And what did I forget?"

"That you said you'd keep what I wrote confidential unless I wrote about something illegal."

Mr. Eikton's face is bright red. "Excuse me," he says to his class.

He steps into the hall and closes the door behind him. My knees are water, and Mrs. Prebyl has caught up with me now.

"You promised you wouldn't report anything if it wasn't illegal. I didn't write anything that should be reported!"

"I'm sorry about this," Mrs. Prebyl says to Mr. Eikton. "Elaine, let's go back to my office and let Mr. Eikton continue with class."

"I wanted to continue with my class," I say. "But of course you didn't care about that."

"That's different, Elaine. You don't have a roomful of students waiting for you."

"Oh, yeah? Go back to the art room and see how many of them are waiting to see what has happened to me since you interrupted to drag me out of class instead of waiting for my study hall!"

I turn back to Mr. Eikton. "Why do you have to keep bringing *her* into this?" I ask, nodding toward Mrs. Prebyl.

"Lainey, I was worried. I was sure that since you didn't write about what happened with Jake, you knew it was something I'd legally have to report."

"Aren't you jumping to conclusions? Both of you? Maybe there was nothing more to say about what happened than what I already wrote, so I wrote something different. Why are you guys so eager to put him away?"

"If Jake did something illegal again," Mrs. Prebyl says, "he may be indicating a need for psychiatric evaluation or residential treatment."

"Residential treatment! Ask him what kind of *treatment* he gets there! Maybe what Jake needs is somebody who thinks he's not *irreparably damaged*!"

I don't know why I suddenly want to protect him. Last night I'd have given anything, absolutely anything, to ship him back to Eldora pronto. I hate Jake's guts, but somehow the fact that everybody gangs up on him and thinks that he'll get *help* in the place that damaged him makes me want to beat my fists against the world's face and scream that Jake isn't always a total loser.

I have to get out of here. If I were in a movie, I'd turn and run out of the building, go find some superhero who could save me, and turn Jake's life around at the same time. But I'm five miles from home and all I can do is whirl on my heel and head back to art class.

They make no move to stop me.

CHAPTER 20

I blew it. That was my chance. Why didn't I just send him away? I can't believe I didn't. I just can't stand the thought of Prebyl the "stone woman" having control of what happens to Jake or pretending to the world that she did it for his good. But if he's locked up, why should I care?

I grab my stuff and slide back onto my stool beside Jailene in art class.

"What was that all about?" she whispers.

"We're both suckers," I mutter at the outlines on my paper that don't look like folds of silk.

Jailene frowns. "Why?"

"You just said yes to another date with Peter, and I just blew my chance to send Jake away."

"You what?"

"We deserve each other as friends, know that?" I smile, wishing I could find it funny. "I just had a chance to put Jake away, to save my own hide—but, no, I stuck up for him."

"Why?" She stops drawing and looks at me.

"I didn't want Prebyl to get her way with him, and I just realized I don't know if I want him sent back there."

"So, you'd rather be dead? Good move, Lainey. You're out of you mind."

"We both are."

"Yeah, but I'm just nuts because two days ago I couldn't remember what I saw in Peter, and now he's got me all tingly again. Love's supposed to be a roller coaster. But you! Holy buckets, Laine, you're gambling with your life."

"I know. But, Jail, I asked how they'd send him back, and they said they'd follow the legal procedures, which could take a couple weeks. If he's going back, that's not good enough. That's not going to help me in time, anyway. I'll be dead by then."

Amy pounces on us when we emerge from the art room. I think she's scared of missing out on something. When she asks what's new in the drama of our lives, Jailene says, "Not much," and we glance at each other. I add, "I'm still alive, and Jailene has another date with Peter on Friday." It seems like years since I was as young as Amy.

.   .   .

Seventh period, Arcadia finds me in the library. We walk behind a bookshelf to talk so Ms. Parker won't ship us out again. I tell her about Pebble Woman and Mr. Eikton.

"Wow, you've got guts to bust into Eikton's class like that."

"No, it was just to get away from Prebyl. I can't stand that woman."

"Why don't you come with me tonight? To stay safe? I'm doing a weight workout, and we could do it together. You could do legs and one arm, anyway. Mom could take you home after work. Or you could stay overnight if you want. I already asked her."

"Bet you didn't tell her why."

"No. She doesn't need to know."

"You lift weights?"

"Yeah, I'm kind of into bodybuilding. My dance teacher got me started, and I like it. I like feeling strong. And it's good for anyone doing sports to be strong. Runners are supposed to lift weights, aren't they?"

"We didn't in junior high, but we're supposed to this year."

"So, want to?"

The idea of working out with Arcadia in a gym

sounds like so much fun, and I consider calling my mom and asking. But I know the answer already, and I need any shred of parental support I can get right now. Something else is bugging me, too. "Hey?" I don't really want to ask this, but she's asked me enough nosy questions that I think I can. "If you're into fitness so much . . ."

"Come on," she says, "out with it. What are you wondering?"

"What was in the thermos you were drinking from the other day? Was it booze? Aren't athletes supposed to stay away from that?"

Her head falls back, hair hanging like silk down her neck, and she laughs so loudly that Ms. Parker barks, "Girls!" from the other side of the bookcase. Arcadia claps her hand over her mouth and her laughter. She's shaking, trying not to make any noise, and catches her balance against the stack of books. "Oh, my God. That's classic."

"Why? What's so funny?"

"Lainey, I bring a protein shake to school every day. Low fat, high protein, the right balance of carbohydrates—to maximize the bodybuilding. But I bring it in a thermos and go over and sit with the druggies 'cause they're more interesting than most people in the cafeteria, and 'cause I *love* the idea that people think I'm drinking something illegal. If *you* thought that, then *everybody* must. I'm surprised Prebyl hasn't been sniffing my thermos yet."

I catch Arcadia's giggles, and it takes every bit of our collective self-control not to burst out laughing.

"I'm sorry," I whisper when we can finally talk.

"Don't be," she says. "It was worth the laugh. So, now that you know I'm not an alcoholic, do you want to come over?" She gives me her big grin.

"Want to? Yeah, I'd sure love to, but I can't. I have to feed my calves, and if it's sunny enough to dry the fields, Dad will be combining, so I'll have to help with all the chores."

"You mean you can never do anything after school again?"

"Just until the babies are big enough to eat solid food and don't need to be nipple-fed. And I'll have cross-country practice again as soon as the doctor says I can run."

"Did I hear you correctly? Did you say 'nipple-fed'?"

I laugh and explain what nipple buckets are.

"Whenever these darling calves outgrow their oral fixation, do you want to start doing weights after school—

or after practice—a couple times a week? If Mom will bring you home?"

"Sure, but you seem to forget that I probably won't be alive long enough to get any benefits from your coaching."

"Well, that perverted little weasel better appreciate your saving him from the Pebble's clutches. You could have delivered him to her, sent him back to the treatment center, and walked away smelling like a rose."

"I haven't saved him. I'm not sure I want to save him. I just didn't want Mrs. Prebyl to win."

The bus ride goes way too fast. I don't want to go home. When we round the last corner and pull onto my paved country road, I can see our big John Deere combine parked beside the drainage ditch where it was last night. Dad's not in the field.

"Mom! Hi!" The screen door slams behind me. No response. "Mom?" I look back out to the barnyard. The pickup is nowhere to be seen. Prickles of fear go up my spine. If I were a dog, my hackles would be up.

I step into the kitchen. There's a note on the table. On impulse, I step back and lock the back door before I even read it.

Lainey—

Went to Granger to get parts for the combine.
Dad tuned it up today and found parts that
needed replacing. I'm going to ride along and get
groceries. Left at 1:30. Please start the chores.
We might be home before you're done, but maybe
not if they're really busy at the implement store.

Love, Mom

P.S. There are chocolate cupcakes on the
pantry shelf. Help yourself.

Cupcakes. My stomach couldn't hold one if they paid me. I have to go out there alone. Maybe I should call the police.

I check all the doors to make sure they're locked, then I go upstairs to change. I step across my room quickly to close my shades. One snaps back up with a pop, and I jump halfway across the room, then I smack it back down on the windowsill again.

I run back downstairs and dig through my backpack and find Arcadia's number. I lean against the kitchen door, letting her phone ring and ring and ring. She's lifting weights, of course, at the gym. I dial Jailene's number. Answering machine. "Jail? It's Lainey. Please call me right away. I'm home alone. Please call me."

I put my chore clothes on and sit on the bed before I can muster the guts to get up and get started. Maybe if I stall long enough, Mom and Dad will come home. They'd rather have no chores done than have no daughter, wouldn't they? Somehow I don't see the humor in my own joke.

Maybe Jailene will call me back before I have to go out. I go downstairs slowly and force myself to eat a cupcake. I even dial Amy's number, but it's busy. It's always busy. She's always online, always, unless she's waiting for me to call. I try Arcadia again—still no answer—and Jailene again, but I don't leave a message this time. I have to go do the chores. It's almost four o'clock.

The sound of my feet on the hardwood floor echoes down the hall. I go to Mom and Dad's bedroom, get down on my hands and knees, lift the bedspread off the floor on Dad's side, and look at his 12-gauge shotgun. I know I can't use that. I only shot it once, and its kick almost knocked me over. I pull it out of the way and get the .22. I have no idea if I can shoot it one-handed.

I take it out of the case and lift it left-handed. I put my left hand on the trigger, prop the barrel on my right forearm above the cast, and aim toward the window shade. I could do it, but it would be very, very slow, and I can't aim well at all because my right arm shakes holding it this way. If I take it to the barn and can't aim, Jake could scare me and I'd shoot some poor sheep or unsuspecting pig or maybe even one of my baby calves.

Dad has a revolver somewhere. He's never let me fire it, but I've seen him use it, and I've watched a lot of movies. I can do it.

I scrounge around and find it in the closet. It's much heavier than I expect, but it's easy to load. Six bullets. I point toward the window, cock it, and try aiming left-handed. At least it's not as heavy as the rifle. I release the hammer slowly and squeeze the trigger slightly until the hammer's back in place, then I place the rifle and shotgun back under the bed.

I try putting the revolver in my pants the way private eyes do, but I can hardly walk, so I grab a belt and slip it in the front of that. It's awkward, but it works. I can manage a left-handed draw.

I head toward the basement, and the phone rings. I jump and slam my shoulder into the doorjamb before I pick up the phone. "Jailene?" I say breathlessly. There's a click, and whoever it is hangs up. My heart is pounding so hard my hand shakes, but I dial Jail's number one more time. This time I leave a message. "Jail, I'm going out to do chores alone. If you get home, tell your mom, okay? I'm scared. If I don't get to talk to you again, good luck with everything. You're a great friend."

I feel stupid as soon as I've said that, but there's no way to retract an answering machine message, so I hang the receiver up. Maybe I should call the cops. But if Dad won't take Jake seriously, why would a police officer?

I stand at the kitchen table for a minute, then I turn over Mom's note and write:

> *Mom and Dad:*
> *I'm scared to go to the barn alone because*
> *Jake is serious about killing me. If I'm gone when*
> *you get here, Jake did something to me. I took*
> *the revolver to try to protect myself. Sorry I did it*
> *without asking.*
> *I love you.*

CHAPTER 21

I hike up my belt and head for the basement. I have to bite the bullet, so to speak. I have to act cool, act like everything's normal—not let Jake see how scared I am. It's my only hope other than Mom and Dad coming home soon or Jailene getting my message. I pull my baggy sweatshirt over the gun and check a mirror. It doesn't show too much.

I fill the buckets with warm water and carry them, one-handed, one-at-a-time, to the barn. I set the first one outside the door, so it can't be opened without moving the bucket. I'm careful not to spill any water, so I can tell if Jake messes with it.

There's not a drop of water on the ground as I bring the last bucket. I can't help looking around as I move the first one out of the way and step into the barn, setting the buckets behind me and latching the door. I wish the doors had locks. Thumper, Bambi, Flower, and Herby bawl like crazy—set off by a combination of hunger and affection—the minute I walk into the barn. I mix the first bucket, rub all four heads, check my gun, and start feeding Flower.

Usually, I talk to the babies the entire time they're slurping and sucking. Today, I'm distracted and jumpy when they nose me. I'm feeding Thumper when Herby bangs his head against the gun; I grab at it with my cast, but I can't keep it from slipping through the belt into the straw on the floor. I don't want to think about what might have happened if it'd been cocked. I bend to grab it as a reflex, jerking Thumper's head. He twists, and the bucket sends a pint of milky spray all over the gun before I realize I can't hold the bucket and pick up the gun at the same time with one hand. I can't hold the bucket with just my cast hand—these little guys suck too hard. I put my feet protectively on either side of the gun while Thumper finishes.

When he's done, I set down the bucket, pick up the gun, wipe it off on my sweatshirt, and put it back in my belt. Jeez. I hope sticky milk won't do any permanent damage. I'm sure Dad will make me clean this tonight. If I'm alive. I can't imagine how much trouble I'm in already.

I feed Herby, and I've just lifted the mix for Bambi

when the barn door bangs. I set the mix down outside the pen and grab the gun out of my belt. Bambi rams his head into my butt. "Hold on, Bambi," I say. I hold the gun in my good hand and survey the barn, trying with my casted hand to keep Bambi from butting me too much. The door is shut.

All the animals are restless because they're getting hungry, so it's hard to detect extra movement or sound that could belong to Jake. The cattle are bunched together at the fence, watching me with hopeful eyes, full of expectation that a human presence means they'll get fed pretty soon, and the sheep are bleating. The pigs have been roused from their naps by the restless sounds of hunger. Under everything else, the Troll's deep voice rolls through the barn. But nothing's as loud as the pounding of my heart. The late sun sends a glow through the dirty west windows, and hay dust dances in the muted sunbeams. Dad's orderly stack of hay and straw bales blocks a clear view of the back door, but everything seems normal.

After a few minutes of watching with Bambi butting me, I put my gun back in my belt, pick up the bucket, brace my backside against the fence and start feeding Bambi. I can still hear my heart thumping over the sucking noise Bambi makes and all the other barn noises.

"Little Miss Smarty-Pants, just couldn't keep her mouth shut, could ya?" Jake's voice is low and even, directly behind me and very close.

I'm too scared to jump. All my cells sort of pop as if they're flash frozen inside the shell of my skin that stays right where it is. I wonder if I look like a big blood blister because everything under my skin has exploded. Bambi yanks his head off the nipple for a split second to see Jake, but when Flower noses in, Bambi butts him in the neck and grabs the nipple again. I don't move, hoping the fact that I didn't jump can be used to my advantage.

"Why'd you have to tell Prebyl, of all people?"

"I didn't!" I say, keeping my back to him, letting Bambi finish. "I wouldn't tell that woman anything, ever." I intend to drop the bucket and whirl around with the gun when I don't have to worry about a sucking calf.

"You think I'm stupid, Lainey-Belainey? What'd you tell Eikton, then?"

"I didn't tell him anything, either, except he figured out that I punched you from something I wrote. That's all."

"Right, and you didn't come barging into his class this afternoon, either."

"I wrote about punching someone. Eikton told me to

finish it with the details about why I did it and what happened. I wouldn't do it. I wrote about something else, so then he took it to Prebyl. She thought I'd left out something illegal to protect you."

"And you did, right?"

"Sort of . . ."

"You're pretty stupid for a smarty-pants, Lainey-Belainey. You can't tell them half stories and expect them not to figure it out. They figure stuff out, they always tell each other stuff, and talk about it behind our backs, come up with their own ideas and go crazy. You're so stupid you need to be put out of your misery."

Bambi is done and starts chewing on the nipple. I pull the nipple away and let the bucket dangle from the elbow on my broken side. I lean over, rubbing the calf's belly and down his front legs until my fingers touch the gun in my belt.

It's time to make my move. I grab the revolver and whirl around, dropping the bucket with a clang and pointing the gun at Jake's voice. He's standing four feet away, with his dad's 12-gauge shotgun leveled at my head. He's got me beat in terms of firepower.

"Lainey-Belainey fights back. Sorry, you don't have a chance, sugar pie." He grins at me with the same steel look in his eyes I've seen before. "My gun's already cocked. You cock yours and you're dead."

I move my thumb onto the hammer. His face looks panicky. "Don't push me, Lainey-Belainey. I'll do it—have to do it since you told. Now, why don't you get out of your calf pen, so I don't have to fight your precious babies off while I clean your brains up from the barn floor?"

I had all sorts of arguments for Jake when I pictured this moment in my head. Now I can't think of any of them. I back toward the fence farthest away from him. In my mind's eye, I can hear the gunshot and see the calves going bonkers in terror, with me crumpling down into their straw.

"Jake," I say. I try to laugh, but it doesn't work. "I thought you were on our porch roof last night."

"I was."

I can't conceal the chill that shoots up my spine and flashes all over my face.

"I climbed down quick when you screamed."

"Were . . . you wearing leather gloves?"

"Yup."

"Oh, God," I say.

"I've been up there a couple times this week. Just biding my time."

"You asshole!" I thumb the hammer on the revolver

back until it's cocked. I want to blow him away.

He looks scared suddenly and levels the gun more carefully at my head. "I didn't want to kill you, Lainey-Belainey, but I guess I have to."

"Jake," I say in desperation, "after you left the roof, you know who came up there? The three-legged squirrel. It's fat and happy and sassy and *fine*! Dad saw it, too, 'cause he woke up when he heard me scream."

"No kidding," he says down his gun barrel. He grins at me. The shotgun barrel is shiny and reflects the white of his teeth all along the length of the gun like some funhouse in a horror movie.

"Jake, maybe you *should* be a vet."

"Huh." He laughs. "I remember Miss Smarty-Pants laughin' her fool head off at that idea when I mentioned it before."

"That was before I knew your surgery was a success." I feel tears in my eyes. I push the only advantage I've got. "That's what I wanted to tell you on the bus when you wouldn't look at me."

"Oh, yeah?"

"Yes, Jake. And I stuck up for you today. When I went into Eikton's room. I was so mad at him for going to Prebyl. And I said you didn't need a treatment center as much as you needed somebody to believe you're not irreparably damaged."

"You said that?"

"Then I just walked away from them. I can't believe I did it, either, because if I hadn't said that, they might have sent you away today. And I wouldn't be lookin' down the barrel of your damn gun."

He lowers his gun a fraction of an inch and can't help the hint of another grin—only in his eyes, not his mouth this time. "Pretty stupid, Lainey-Belainey. You blew your chance. 'Course, you should have thought of all that when you started tellin' the whole world."

"Jake, I didn't . . ."

"Don't lie to me. Amy, Jailene, that preacher's daughter, your mom, and of course your everlastin' dad. My dad says we get kicked off the place if I show up here again, you know that?"

I nod and swallow. "That means you're kicked off now."

"If he sees me. So you think I'm ir-repair-able?"

"I don't know, Jake. Are you gonna shoot me? That's irreparable. But while you rot in jail or wherever, wishing you were in veterinary school, you can remember I stood up for you but you shot me anyway."

"I'll remember you were the one who sent me away!"

We eyeball each other, then Jake asks, "Lainey-Belainey, have you ever wanted to have sex with anybody?"

"Why?"

"I wanna know. Tell me."

"Maybe Keanu Reeves. Or Tiger Woods."

"Why didn't you want to have sex with me?"

"I'm not going to do it with just anybody."

"I'm just anybody?"

"I mean, we're just friends. Or we were friends once. I want to be in love."

He snorts. "Know a lot about sex for a smarty-pants virgin, don't ya, Lainey-Belainey?"

"I don't know, Jake," I say. "That's just what I think. That's what I want. I s'pose it could be lots different when it really happens."

"Could be *lots* different," Jake says. He steps toward me, lowering his gun. I hold mine, pointing it at his chest. He swings his legs over into the calf pen, and I back up against the farthest gate of the pen, my left arm extended with the gun.

"I could rape ya here," Jake says.

"You do, and I'll kill you."

"Let me finish, smarty-pants. I could rape you right here, right now, and you might like it. Might love it. It's not something you can know until it happens."

"You're sick, Jake. Nobody likes to be raped, you moron."

"You've got a lot to learn, Lainey-Belainey. You just don't know until it happens." He takes another step toward me. "I could—"

"Don't take another step, Jake Riley." The gun's getting so heavy, I have to keep lifting it so it stays pointed at him.

"But I won't. I wouldn't do that." He stops where he is, lowering his gun to hip level. "I'd never do that to anyone."

"What? You'd kill me, but you wouldn't rape me?"

"I don't want to hurt you. Never wanted to. I just didn't know what to say when you found me in the calf pen. Thought I'd have to put you out of your stupid misery to save my own hide, so I wouldn't get sent back there for *that*, but I didn't want to hurt you."

I frown at him.

"Remember how I stopped before, when you said no?"

"You never stopped! I got away."

"Well, I would have stopped. You didn't give me a chance. I never chased ya, did I?"

"You can't run fast enough to catch me!"

We stare at each other over our loaded guns, then Jake says, "When I first went in, I used to cry at night. I missed my mom. I was only eleven. There was this real skinny kid—Slat, they used to call him, but his name was really something else, Matt, I think. He found me crying in the bathroom one night, and he was real nice to me. He asked if I wanted him to do something to me that would make me feel better."

I feel the gun getting heavier in my left hand. The trigger's sweaty, and I lower it a little bit. It's still cocked.

Jake's eyes flicker at me and then away.

"I couldn't *believe* how good it felt, what he did to me. I didn't have a clue what he was doing. I'd never even masturbated before, so it was like magic."

We're quiet a minute, then Jake says, "You can't tell this to anybody if you're dead, you know."

"I know." My lips are dry like pieces of balsa wood rubbing together.

"I jerked off, but it wasn't as good. So then I found out that if you did somebody else, they'd do you. Or if you were bigger than somebody else, you could get them to do you in trade for protecting them."

"Why are you telling me this?" I ask.

"'Cause it ain't always the way you think it's gonna be. I hated the *idea* of it, see, but I liked *doin'* it. And I'm tellin' you 'cause I never lied to you, 'cept when I said the bigger boys made me do it at Eldora. Nobody ever forced me. I liked it."

I can hear myself swallow.

"So I think I might be gay. Or maybe not. I sure like the looks of girls, but I've never had the chance. Until you. I thought maybe if I liked it with you, it would mean I just like sex with girls, and that's normal, and everything else was just gettin' me ready for the real thing."

I think about Arcadia's dad's theory about teenage boys and sex, and I'm sure he's right. I lower my gun another millimeter.

"Those boys," Jake says, still looking down, "they were my friends. I never hated them. We just had a secret together. So I didn't think it would make you hate me. And you were my only friend here, so getting you to do it seemed like—like what I was used to."

"Guess you blew it."

"Forever?"

"Well, what do you think? You shoot me, and you blow it forever. You scare me shitless so I'll never trust you again, and you've blown it anyway."

"I don't want no double-crossing friends. Friends don't tell stuff."

"Friends don't threaten to kill their friends."

"So why'd you make me do this? Why'd you lie to me and sneak up on me and tell people I'm a murderer?" He pulls his gun up to his shoulder. Now there are real tears in his eyes. "It's your fault. I need to kill you, Lainey-Belainey. After you started tellin' your mom and dad that I'm a murderer, I thought I might as well be one."

I close my eyes, 'cause I'll be dead before I can pull my trigger. I feel everything around me going away, that it's all over, and I hate the tears I feel under my eyelids.

I wait, but I finally hear Jake's voice again instead of a blast.

"One more thing. I was in for *manslaughter*, Lainey-Belainey, not *murder*. There's a big difference, stupid. Don't you know the difference? You've been tellin' everybody that I was in for murder, and I wasn't."

"I thought . . . you said . . ."

"I said manslaughter. If I was in for murder, I wouldn't have been the scared little kid in there. But it wasn't murder, I mean, it was an accident."

"It . . . what? What happened?"

"I got in a fight," Jake says, watching me down the sight of the shotgun. He moves the gun like a gesture so it sort of circles around my head. "With my mom's boyfriend. He was psycho. He was so dumb, the son of a—" He bites his lip so hard I expect it to start bleeding.

"Mom was at work, and the jerk was going to stay at our house—he was always there. I locked the apartment door at night, like always. There was the key lock in the knob, and then there was a chain lock like in hotel rooms, you know?"

I nod.

"At about ten o'clock, we were watching TV, and the fire alarms went off. I barely looked up, because kids were pulling the fire alarms all the time and it was no big deal. But he always had to be the hero, always had to be in the middle if something big was going on, so just in case it's a fire and he would need to be a hero, he ran to the door and jerked it open. The whole damn door frame splintered apart on the side with the chain. I heard it crack, like a big bone breaking, and I ran to see what happened.

"So he started swearing like a madman, then he stuck his head out and ran down the hall. In his underwear! When he couldn't find any smoke, he came back, shut the door, and looked at me like he'd kill me.

"'Why'd you make me do that?' he asked me.

"I said, 'I didn't do anything. You broke the door.'

"'Why the hell didn't you tell me the door was chained? You made me break the goddam door.'

"I thought it was funny that he said it was my fault, but then I realized he really wanted to hurt me. He whipped out his belt and started swingin' it at me, yellin', 'You shrimpy bastard! The place could have been on fire! Why didn't you tell me you chained it?' He smacked me really hard with the belt buckle a few times—once in the ear, and it was bleeding, and once on my backbone, and it hurt like crazy—and finally I got in my room and slammed the door."

Jake's gun has been lowering slowly. Now it's about waist high. I let my gun relax, too. The calves are nestling into the straw around our feet.

"He was outside yellin' that he'd rip the door of my room off the hinges to give me what I deserved, and I knew he could do it. I was scared, so I got my baseball bat to get ready for him in case he broke that door down, too. Pretty soon, *wham*, he came flyin' through the door, and I brought the bat down, *bam*, on his head. And he's gone, out like a light. I stood there, waiting for him to come to, glad I beat him, then scared that I killed him.

"I called Mom and said he was out cold, and she said to let him sleep it off. But then I told her what happened, and she went crazy, so I called nine-one-one. She spent the night in the hospital with *him*, while *I* was at the police station. I hit him in a bad spot, and a blood clot killed him, so I got juvenile involuntary manslaughter. Mom was more worried about the guy who was trying to kill me than she was about me.

"And nobody wants you in a foster home if you've killed somebody, so I got sent to Eldora, and here I am. That was three years ago."

He hefts his gun in one hand. "So I reckon I could kill you, too, if I needed to protect myself. Now that ya know all that, I really ought to kill ya."

I hate the barrel end of a gun.

"Jake, come on." I shake my revolver to remind him we're nearly even. "You don't have to do this."

"Yeah, I do." There are tears coming down his cheeks now. "I didn't mean to kill him, but what would you have done? I just hit him. You hit me to protect yourself and your calves. Am I a criminal, Lainey? What would you have done? You would have done the same thing, wouldn't you?"

"I—I don't know."

"Yes, you do! Tell me!" He points the gun at me and I feel tears, too. I lift my revolver, and I touch the hammer with my thumb to make sure it's cocked. Just as my finger touches the trigger, there's a blast that shakes my arm, my whole body, ripping through the barn. I feel it more than hear it, and the flash makes me think I'm dying. I can see Jake jumping, falling backward over the fence, out onto the aisle of the barn.

"Jake!" I hear myself screaming, but my voice is far away through the ringing of my ears from the gun blast. My God, I shot Jake.

"Jake, Jake, Jake!" I can't stop screaming. I scramble over the gate through the dust and chaff and haze to Jake, who's sitting up in the aisle, his face as white as calf formula, staring past me toward the barn door. His hair is coated with hay dust and his lips are moving, but I don't hear anything, and for a second I think it's because he's dying, but I don't see any blood. He's staring over my shoulder and as I turn to look, I stumble and topple over in the straw beside Jake.

Through the haze of the falling chaff and dust, Dad is walking toward us like a figure emerging from the mist in a graveyard, holding his double-barreled 12-gauge, fixing Jake with a look that's more terrible than I knew he could wear. I didn't shoot Jake. Dad fired a double-barreled blast that either blew Jake backward or scared him off his feet. My thinking is in slow motion, and I still can't hear anything.

Dad's lips are moving. Then I see the veins in his neck bulging, and I know he's yelling. His lips are saying, "Lainey, move out of the way, get out of the way!"

I get up and run to him. "Dad, stop!" I feel myself scream, and I can hear a tiny bit of my voice around the edges of the ringing in my ears. He read the note. I forgot about the note, forgot about Mom and Dad coming home, forgot all about the time. He didn't believe me, but now he came to save me, to do whatever it took to save me. And now it's Jake that needs saving.

We turn and there's Jake on the barn floor, arms around his knees, shaking like a leaf with the shotgun several feet away in the straw. Dad's shotgun is still pointed in Jake's direction. I run to Jake and scream toward his ear, "Did he shoot you? Are you okay?"

"He missed me," Jake's mouth says to me. "On purpose."

There's a big hand on my shoulder, and Dad pulls me away from him. I can almost hear Dad's voice: "Are you okay? Are you sure you're okay?"

I nod. "Yes." I grab his arm. "Put your gun away, please."

I sit down on the straw across from Jake, and Dad sits on the gate, shotgun across his lap. We're quiet for several minutes. The animals around us fill the emptiness with hungry noises. Finally, I realize I'm hearing again.

"Did you really think I'd kill you?" Jake asks me.

"What else could I think? You did everything to make me think you would. And you were up on my goddam roof! Dad, Jake *was* on the roof last night."

Dad's eyes narrow at me. "Lainey, I thought you were really going crazy."

"I just wanted to scare you bad, Lainey. I never wanted to kill you," Jake says, still shaking.

"If you weren't serious, you need a psychiatrist for pointing a loaded gun at my daughter's face. I didn't believe you really wanted to kill her until I walked into the barn tonight."

Jake crawls over to his shotgun and hands it to Dad. Dad pops open the chamber. "It's not loaded," he says.

Jake shakes his head and starts to cry. "I just wanted to scare you really bad, so you wouldn't tell, so I wouldn't go back there."

"Jake," Dad says, "I think you have to go back. This is a farm. This isn't a counseling service or a rehab center. I know how to make rules and how to make you work, but I don't know what the hell to do with someone who breaks my rules and climbs on my roof and looks in my daughter's window, someone who threatens my daughter's life."

"And I told your dad that if you came in our barnyard one more time, you'd be out. This is it. You point a gun at my daughter's face, you're out. No more chances."

Jake nods. He understands perfectly. He just leans his face into the knees of his jeans and cries some more. Finally, he lifts his head up and says, "Everybody will know. Everybody will hate me. Nobody will let us live by them. I guess I have to go back there."

"Jake," I say, "what you told me about why you were in Eldora, and what it was like, it's not fair. None of it is fair."

"Doesn't matter," Jake says. He wipes his nose on his jacket sleeve. "Fair doesn't have anything to do with it."

I lean my head back against the gate and look up into the still drifting hay dust. "Look!" I point up. No wonder the hay dust is so thick. Over our heads, there's a gaping, splintery hole that the shotgun made in the floor of the haymow.

CHAPTER 22

Dad sends Jake home, and I help him finish choring. We don't talk at all, and I feel pretty shaky. We step out of the barn just as a car drives in. It's Jailene.

Jail practically falls out of the car before it comes to a stop.

"What happened?" she yells at me. I run to hug her. I'm so glad to see her, so glad she's my friend. I blurt out what happened.

"I was *so* scared," she says. "I can't tell you how scared!"

"*You* were scared!" I say. I drag her over by the garden so we can talk better. I tell her the rest of the details about Jake.

"Wow," she says. "The only part that's really his fault is what he did to you." She looks at me. "Which is plenty."

Mom invites them to stay for supper, but Jail's mom

has to get home to feed the rest of her family.

"Peter called when we were leaving," Jail whispers as she's getting in the car. "He wanted to see me tonight."

"So why are you here?" I ask.

"Priorities," she says and grins at me.

"Thanks."

Before supper, I tell Mom and Dad the whole story. Dad calls Raymond and says they'll get together in the morning to talk about what will have to happen. Raymond and Jake will have the evening to talk together.

"Raymond," Dad says when he gets off the phone, "is mortally embarrassed and says the only thing he can do now is leave."

"I should think so," Mom says.

I feel bad, really bad. At the same time, I don't want Jake next door. I never, ever, want to worry that someone is outside my window in the middle of the night.

After cleaning up the supper dishes, I call Arcadia, but her mom says she's not home. "Is she at the gym?" I ask.

"Yes, she is. She said she was worried about something and needed to work off the stress. Is this Lainey?" she asks.

"Yeah, why?"

"Because it was you she was worried about."

"Well, can you please tell her I tried to call when I needed her and she was too busy working off her stress to be of any help."

Her mom doesn't know what to say to that.

"I'm kidding. Sort of. It's funny now, but it wasn't a few hours ago. Anyway, tell her what I said about being too busy working off her stress to help when I needed it, okay? And tell her everything sort of worked out tonight. I'll fill her in tomorrow."

It feels good to go to bed without being afraid for once, but it still takes me a long time to sleep.

Then, sometime in the night, I wake up dreaming I hear noises on the porch roof outside my window. But it's not a dream—it's a real noise. I get up and my heart thumps, even though I tell myself it's just the squirrel again. I go to the window and open my mouth to scream. There's Jake, holding his finger over his mouth for me to be quiet. I clamp my hand over my mouth. He motions for me to open the window, and I open it just enough so I can hear him but not far enough for him to try to get in.

"What do you want? Are you insane? Dad missed

the first time," I hiss. "He wouldn't miss again!"

"I came to say good-bye," Jake says. "I can't stay here anymore. Everybody will hate me, and they'll hear what happened, even if you don't tell anybody. Plus, if I go away, my dad can stay here and keep his job."

"Jake, where are you going?"

He looks at me, straight in the eye. "Somewhere I can take care of ir-repair-able stuff. You know. Only one thing to do if something's ir-repair-able."

"Jake! What do you mean?" I'm sure that I know what he means, and I scan him for a hidden gun. "No, Jake, don't . . . Don't do that, Jake. Please!"

"Lainey, if I'm still here, Dad has to move . . . or they will send me back to Eldora. Neither one of those things is okay. So I just need to take myself out of the picture. That's all I'm doin', Lainey."

"Jake, you can't *just die*, after all this . . ."

He looks me in the eye. "Yeah, I can, actually."

"Jake, I'm gonna scream if you're gonna shoot yourself. They'll stop you. You don't have to *die.*"

"Lainey, settle down."

"What *are* you gonna do, Jake? And why are you here?"

"I wanted . . ."

"What?"

"I wanted to say I'm sorry."

I think about the one other time he apologized, after pulling up my shirt, when I made him say why he was sorry. I look at his face, and I know I don't need to ask why this time.

"Apology accepted."

"Well, bye then." He backs away from the window, but I throw the window up farther and slide the screen up its track so I can stick my head and arms out the window. I slide halfway out and reach around him to give him a big hug. My eyes are burning.

He lets me hug him, but he doesn't seem to know how to hug me back. He awkwardly puts his hands around my shoulders, too.

Then he backs out of the hug, toward the edge of the roof, where he stops and looks at me. "Thanks, Lainey-Belainey. Nobody has hugged me since Mom."

I watch him go down the drainpipe out of sight, one hand last like the night before.

I drag a blanket off my bed and sit for a long time by the window, listening to the leaves, dry and rattling in the night breeze, the hum of grain dryers, and the distant buzz of traffic on the interstate a mile away.

Just when I'm ready to crawl back into bed, I hear semi brakes hiss through the blackness. That's odd.

There's no reason for a truck to stop on the interstate within hearing distance. No exit ramps, no weigh stations, and not even any curves through the flat Iowa land. But the sound is definitely air brakes, like the honk of a mammoth goose, being deflated a mile away. That doesn't make sense unless something is on the highway.

Something like a hitchhiker. That's it. My heart stops in my throat. He did it. Through the stillness, I can hear the semi rev its engine and start again, heading up the highway. I imagine Jake slamming himself into the cab, flashing a jack-o'-lantern grin at the driver. I wish I could cry, but I just sit staring, listening to the faint sound of the motor disappearing north, into the blackness.

I wait and wait for sunup, watching for the squirrel who wasn't irreparable after all.

I wonder if he'll come back.